THE SANTA RULES

A HOLIDAY ROM COM

MYA MORE

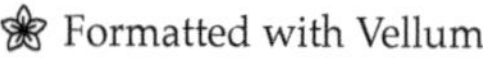 Formatted with Vellum

For all the moms just trying to survive the holidays. May your coffee be strong, your kids be well-behaved, and your stocking be fully stuffed. 😌

But most importantly, I hope the ladies stay in place if you ever sleep in a tank top.

CONTENT WARNINGS

Light impact play (spanking)
Hand necklace
Loss of a spouse (mentioned)
Loss of a parent (mentioned)
Alcoholism (not a main character)
Fire in an occupied school
Crass boy mom humor, including puberty jokes

You know your limits and triggers. Your mental health is important.

Any scenes with kink depicted in this book are for entertainment purposes and are not intended to be educational or accurate depictions of a BDSM/kink lifestyle. Please do your research before engaging in similar acts to make sure you are your partner(s) are informed and safe.

DICKTIONARY 🌶️

For anyone wondering where the steamy scenes take place—whether you're eager to dive right in or prefer to skip them altogether—you'll find them in the following chapters:

🌶️ Chapter 7
🌶️ Chapter 10
🌶️ Chapter 11
🌶️ Chapter 17
🌶️ Chapter 19
🌶️ Bonus Chapter (download)

PLAYLIST ♫

Underneath the Tree - Kelly Clarkson
Silent Night - Teddy Swims
Star On Top - Pentatonix
Santa Tell Me - Ariana Grande
Snowman - Sia
Let it Snow! Let it Snow! Let it Snow! - Dean Martin
Chestnuts by the Fire - Copamore
Christmas In Hollis - Run–D.M.C
santa doesn't know you like i do - Sabrina Carpenter
Jingle Bells - Remastered - Frank Sinatra
The Christmas Song (Chestnuts Roasting On an Open Fire) - Martina McBride
Mistletoe - Justin Bieber
What Christmas Means to Me - John Legend, Stevie Wonder
Merry Christmas, Happy Holidays - *NSYNC
It's Beginning to Look a Lot Like Christmas - Michael Bublé
One More Sleep - Leona Lewis
You Make It Feel Like Christmas - Gwen Stefani, Blake Shelton
Man With The Bag - Jessie J
O Holy Night - Céline Dion
Merry Christmas - Ed Sheeran, Elton John

Christmas Without You - Ava Max
Santa, Can't You Hear Me - Kelly Clarkson, Ariana Grande
My Favorite Things - Pentatonix
Santa Claus Is Coming To Town - The Jackson 5
All I Want for Christmas Is You - Mariah Carey
Here Comes Santa Claus - Pentatonix
Yippee Ki Yay - Marco Beltrami
Christmas Cookies - RuPaul
Let it Snow - Boyz II Men, Brian McKnight
Silent Night - Pentatonix

CHAPTER 1
BELLA

"Jesus, Mom, your tits are out!" Isaac screams in disgust.

I look down, and sure as fuck, he's right. My right breast has made its escape out of the side of my tank top, while Lefty has jumped ship out of the top.

"It's not like these babies didn't provide you nourishment for the first two years of your life," I grumble. Why I feel the need to fight with my thirteen-year-old at this early hour is beyond me. Groaning, I sit up in bed and pull my tank top up to cover the girls.

"Please don't refer to your tits as babies," he whines.

I should have more fucks to give, but parenting a thirteen-year-old boy alone has left me fresh out of fucks. And snacks. And hot water. And lotion. And my sanity.

I'm probably going to scar him for life between the tit flashing and the inappropriate jabs I level at him. But I'm doing the best I can. The lemonade may not be as sweet as I'd like, but dammit, I've squeezed the hell out of the lemons life's thrown at me.

"It's too fucking early in the morning for you to be coming at me like you have a full set of pubes."

He leaves the room in a huff, and I fall back on the bed,

hoping to get a few more winks in before we need to leave for school. But a few minutes later, he throws open my door, startling me as he marches back in, looks me square in the eyes, and says, "Twelve."

I blink at him in confusion. "What are you talking about?"

This kid crosses his arms over his chest in defiance and glances down at his crotch.

"Oh my God, you didn't," I squeak out between fits of laughter.

"I have twelve hairs down there."

"Did you actually count?"

He levels a glare at me, trying to be menacing, but it's impossible. There's no way to look tough when you just counted your pubic hairs in an attempt to win an argument with your mom. I collapse into a fit of laughter.

"Whatever. I'm going to go make some breakfast."

"Let me know if you need a scrunchie to hold all that hair! Don't want to get any in your Frosted Flakes!" I call after him.

"Shut up!"

"I love you too!"

Once Isaac is ready, we head out the door and walk over to Chestnut Mountain K-12 School. Isaac heads to his homeroom, and I stop by the office to check my mailbox and then make my way to my kindergarten classroom.

I shut the door behind me and inhale a deep breath as I try to prepare for what is sure to be an exhausting day. It's Friday, there's a full moon, and it's one of the few days of the year when the kids are allowed to dress up and eat candy. There's not a teacher I know that likes Halloween. Sure, they may like it at home, but not in their classroom. Kids are hopped up on sugar, no one can sit still, and forget about teaching anything because no one can focus with all the Spider-Men, Stormtroopers, princesses, witches, and other various ghouls and goblins running around. Me included.

It does make me miss the days when Isaac liked dressing

up. He's too cool for that now, but he is good with kids, and my students love when he comes to visit. I shouldn't have teased him this morning—I may need his help wrangling this chaos later.

There's so much I enjoy about teaching, but lately it's been hard to keep up, and I feel like I'm failing at everything. With only one of me, I'm stretched thin—between all the paperwork at school, all the paperwork my kid brings home, and all the paperwork my mailman keeps bringing me, it's too much to keep up with. And that's just the paper.

After way too many sugar crashes, one very sticky Batman, and a farting incident that derailed story time for thirty minutes, I'm exhausted when I walk in my house later that night, and I need something to help me relax.

"I'm gonna play with my friends then head to bed," Isaac says as he climbs the stairs to his gaming cave, otherwise known as his bedroom. I'm probably a shit mom for letting him have a computer in his room, but he's a good kid and I trust him. Plus, his dad bought it for him, and I didn't really have much say in that matter.

While I wait for him to crash, I grab the empty candy bowl off the porch and scroll through a hookup app on my phone. Okay, now I'm definitely a shit mom, but it's been six months since I've had a good manhandling, and I need it after today.

An hour later, Brandon shows up and I sneak him into my room, locking the door behind us as we furiously paw at each other. He's a little too timid with his tongue for my liking.

"We have to be quiet. My kid is down the hall," I whisper while removing Brian's belt. Or was it Brad? Who the fuck cares?

"Shit, you have a kid?" He pauses after removing my bra from under my shirt.

"Don't worry, he's not yours."

Brian chuckles. "Clearly." He glances around the room,

almost as if he expects my kid to pop out and scare him. "Look…"

I push him back on the bed before he can shut this down. "No, *you* look. I need this. I need to feel the weight of a man on my body while he plows me from behind because that's not something I can easily recreate with my vibrator. Okay, Brady?"

"It's Brandon."

"I don't care." I work at the buttons on his jeans, pulling them open. "I'm sure you're a nice guy, but we both know what this is. One night. I'm not asking you to be a stepdad. I just want to fuck, and I don't want my kid to know you're here."

A dull pain throbs in my core, but I ignore it, grabbing his erection through his boxers. "Fuck," he groans, his head dropping back on the bed. "I don't have any condoms."

Is he for real? "We met on DTF, Bradley—"

"Brandon."

"Whatever. The app is called Down to Fuck. How did you not come prepared?"

"Uhhh…I'm clean?" He offers the last part like it's a question he hopes I have the answer to instead of a statement that inspires confidence.

"Cool. Need help putting this on, Brayden?" I retort, tossing a condom at him that I found in my nightstand.

"Brandon!" he says, as I reach for the waistband of his jeans. That dull throb in my core builds into something more as he continues. "You're really hot, and I can't believe I'm going to say this, but I'm going to take a raincheck." He hops up off the bed and refastens his pants.

"I think that's—AHHHHH," I groan as a sudden sharp, stabbing pain hits my abdomen and I double over.

"Uhhh, are you okay?"

"No" is all I manage to squeak out as I clutch at my side.

Spots dot my vision as I collapse on the floor. I can hear

Benton talking, but I can't make out what he's saying. It sounds like he's in a tin can really far away. Holy shit, am I dying?

"Uhhh, she's like in her thirties, I think?" I hear him walk out of the room. "Let me look. I don't remember the address."

The next thing I know, I'm on my back with a bright light shining in my eyes.

"Ma'am, can you hear me?"

My eyes blink rapidly at a man I don't know in my room. "Yeah," I croak out, clutching at my side. The pain is over-whelming. Is it my appendix? A kidney stone? Fate stepping in to save me from a bad lay?

"My name is Hardy. Your husband called 911. We're here to help."

"Not her husband. I'm going to take off. Looks like you guys have this covered," the coward calls as I hear him descend the stairs.

"Assho—" I start before another wave of stabbing pain sears my abdomen. "Fuck."

"Ma'am, can you tell us what's going on?"

"Stabbing pains. Down here." I gesture to the area above my pubic bone.

"Does it hurt anywhere else? Any other symptoms?"

"Oh God, I'm gonna throw up," I wail as I curl onto my side, a wave of sweat beading down my face.

A blue vomit bag is placed close to my mouth as a hand soothes circles on my back.

Please don't let me vomit in front of a stranger.

Is this food poisoning? I wrack my brain trying to think of everything I ate today. It was mostly candy. Did I finally find the piece of candy our parents warned us about? The one laced with drugs that we were always told to check for? Is this how I'm going to die? Taken out by poisoned candy?

There's no way to look graceful while writhing on the floor dry heaving into a bag. As quickly as it hits, the nausea subsides, and I try to sit up. "Thanks, I think it passed." I hold out the vomit bag, unable to look at the man helping me.

"Can you verify your name and date of birth?"

"Bella, with two Ls, last name Carlisle," I divulge before reciting my birthdate, even though I'm less than thrilled about sharing it. A lady never tells. And based on this evening's activities, I am clearly a lady. Cue eye roll.

"Are you able to walk to the ambulance, or do we need to wheel you out?" another EMT I didn't even realize was here asks as the first one helps me sit up. Does he have an accent or did I hit my head?

"I can walk, but I might need some help." I refuse to make eye contact with either of them as humiliation burns my cheeks.

"I got you." An arm snakes around my waist and hoists me up as I groan out in pain. "That okay?"

"Yes, I'm sorry. It hurts." I want to die of mortification. No one ever sees me this vulnerable.

"No need to apologize. That's what we're here for."

I groan as we slowly descend the stairs. "Shit. Isaac."

"Do you need me to call someone?" asks the paramedic who's holding me up.

"It's my kid. He's in his room. Gaming." I'm not surprised that he hasn't emerged since he usually wears noise-cancelling headphones while he plays. Mother of the year here.

"Do you have anyone that can watch him? A neighbor, maybe?"

"His dad?" I suggest, but I already know that won't happen. When it's not his weekend, Jake is practically unreachable.

"Let me get you loaded up, then we can get him sorted."

I refuse to look at his face because I can tell from the deep, gravelly voice that this man is attractive. We make it out to my front yard, and I spot the stretcher a few feet in front of me. I reach out, groping for it, as tears stream down my cheeks. The pain is excruciating, and I can't stop apologizing as the EMT helps me onto the stretcher. I'm the one who helps other people; I'm not used to others helping me. Very few people in my life are reliable, so I've learned to depend on myself.

The stretcher is much harder than it looks, making lying on my back unpleasant. Shifting onto my hip takes some effort, but I successfully curl up on my left side, one hand clutching my torso while the other rests under my head. The feeling of something warm and fleshy against my arm sets off alarm bells in my head, but I forget about that when I lock eyes with the most handsome man I have ever seen. His eyes dart around as if unsure where to look while he talks into a device strapped to his shoulder, calling out my vitals as he leans over me, securing me to the stretcher.

I'm jostled down my driveway toward the ambulance, and I pinch my eyes shut in pain as I try to take a deep breath. Nope, that hurts. I can hear hushed voices, and when I open my eyes, I see old Mrs. Johnson across the street pointing at me with one hand while the other clasps her signature pearl necklace. She is literally clutching her pearls.

And when I look down, I see why.

Fuck my life.

That warm, fleshy thing I felt on my arm earlier was my breast. My whole left breast is out of my shirt. Lefty decided this was when she would escape her fabric confines and seek freedom with the wind in her hair. Fuck, I hope there's no nipple hair on display that I forgot to pluck. Oh my God, I want to die. The hot EMT saw my whole tit and probably my errant nipple hair. And now Mrs. Johnson will probably tell all of Chestnut Mountain.

My sweet, older, next door neighbor Cora calls out, "Don't worry, Bella, I'll watch Isaac for you," as the hot EMT loads me into the ambulance.

"Still need me to call someone?"

"If she can stay with him, that's fine."

He climbs out of the ambulance to talk to Cora briefly before hopping back in and closing the doors.

"She said she can stay with him till you get home," Hardy says as he noticeably avoids eye contact.

Because my tit is still exposed, I make an attempt to reach Lefty and tuck her back in her polyester prison, but I can't due to the straps holding me down.

"Um, Hardy? That's what you said your name was, right?" This is humiliating.

"Yes, ma'am."

"You can stop calling me ma'am."

"Okay, Bella. I'm going to need to take your blood pressure again. Can you straighten this arm?" he asks, tapping on the left elbow of the arm that is folded under my head. The one my tit is propped up on.

"Sure," I reply. It all happens in slow motion. My arm extends out just as he stands and leans over me to grab the blood pressure cuff. He's at the right angle, and the back of my hand grazes down the front of his pants, smoothing along the bulge in his crotch. The rather large bulge.

"Shit, I'm so sorry!" I say. Why can't I do anything right? I can't even hook up with a guy without it ending in disaster. This is the second dick my hand has grazed tonight, and yet I'm no closer to ending my dry spell. Why am I such a hot mess?

"It's fine. I'm just going to loosen these straps so you can lie flat on your back while I check your vitals."

The overhead lights in this vehicle are blinding as I lie back against the hard gurney. Hardy places the cuff on my arm while another EMT grabs my right arm and begins tying an elastic around it. Where did he come from? I didn't hear him get in the ambulance.

Both of my arms are preoccupied, and Lefty still has her head out of the window, tongue flapping in the breeze.

"Hardy, can you do me a favor and put my tit back in my

shirt, please?" I turn to the other guy. "Sorry, I don't know your name, or I would've asked you."

IV guy smiles. "No worries, it's Mike," he says, shooting Hardy a smirk. Yup, he definitely has an accent. Irish maybe?

There's some tugging on my neckline, and I once again feel the fabric covering my escape artist.

"All covered."

"Thanks. How long was it out?" I ask.

"Since the moment I arrived on the scene."

"Well, that's humiliating."

I wince in embarrassment and from the death grip EMT Mike has on my arm. "I'm having trouble getting a vein to cooperate on this arm. You wanna try the left?"

"Sure," Hardy says, taking all the implements from him.

"Oh shit. Shit, shit, shit." I cringe and ball my fist. I hate needles, and we're in the back of a moving vehicle. These mountain roads are known for sharp curves and potholes, and I just know I'm going to end up getting stabbed. This is how I'm going to die, with these nice men trying to save me.

Squeezing my eyes closed, I try to take calming breaths, but it feels like I'm hyperventilating, and I'm getting lightheaded.

"Her heart rate is elevated," Mike says, but his voice sounds distant.

A warm hand strokes my head. "Alright, Bella, I need you to breathe," Hardy commands, looking into my eyes. "That's it. Deep breaths. In and out. That's it. Good girl." His eyes flick over to the monitor, then back to me. "Good to know all it takes is a little praise to calm you down."

Is he flirting with me?

I take a moment to examine his features. Full lashes surround crystal blue eyes as he peers at me with concern. His thick eyebrows are pinched together in concentration. He smells like smoke and something manly. There's a light dusting of a five-o'clock shadow covering his hard jaw that matches the color of his chocolate brown hair. And his lips. Fuck me, those are thick, full, kissable lips.

"IV's in," Hardy says, and I blink in surprise as I look down at my arm.

"Holy shit, I didn't even feel it."

"What every guy loves to hear," Mike jokes.

Hardy scowls at his partner. "Oh, she'd feel it if I wanted her to feel it."

Are we still talking about the needle?

"Can confirm. I definitely felt *it*." I smile as I think about all the things I want to feel on him.

My eyes do a slow perusal of his body, zeroing in on the way his pants tighten across his lap. He reaches down to adjust himself, and a warm flush passes through my body. It could be the pain medication taking effect, or it could be the way the hot paramedic is staring at me. Like he wants to devour me.

Am I imagining that?

When we arrive at the hospital, there's a flurry of movement, and I lose track of Hardy in the shuffle.

After several hours and two bottles of water, I'm finally able to collect a urine sample only to find out I have a bad bladder infection. The meds they gave me are already kicking in, giving me a second wind when I walk in the door in the wee hours of the morning, thanks to my friend Lucy who drove me home. Cora is sitting at my kitchen table with a cup of coffee waiting for me.

"Thank you," I groan as I sink into the chair and inhale the aroma. "All that, and it was just a bladder infection. I appreciate you staying with Isaac."

"It's no problem, dear. He was asleep for most of it. I can stay a little longer if you want to get some rest," Cora says as she squeezes my arm. She's been really sweet since we moved in here after my divorce four years ago, helping watch Isaac from time to time.

"I'm fine. I was able to get a little sleep while waiting on the doctor, and I'm oddly wired from the experience and the meds. I want to put away all these Halloween decorations anyway."

After flashing Mrs. Johnson, the last thing I need is her stirring up more gossip. If I can put my decorations away in a timely manner, maybe she'll see that I'm not the disaster everyone thinks I am.

"You don't have to do it all alone, you know. Want some help?"

"That's really sweet of you, but I wouldn't feel right putting you out anymore."

"Nonsense, you're giving this old lady something to do. Keeps my mind sharp. And we're a community. Chestnut Mountain may be small, but we help our own."

"Think it's too early to put out all my Christmas decor? I could really use some holiday magic right now." Christmas was my mom's favorite holiday, and I always miss her most around this time of year. "Maybe it'll shut Mrs. Johnson up if she sees that I already have my holiday decor up."

"Oh, I know it will." There's a mischievous glint in her eye as she speaks. "That's why we should definitely do it. That woman runs her mouth more than a parrot in a pet store."

"I wish all my neighbors were as cool as you."

Even though it's five a.m., we start taking down spiders, cobwebs, and cornstalks, and replace them with projector lights, way too many Santas, and a half dozen inflatables. I try to get a new one each year, but my options are limited in the after-Christmas sales because it's hard to go all out on a teacher's budget. I've learned to be resourceful by saving everything and shopping clearance sales.

It's no Griswold light display, but it sends the message to my grinch of a neighbor: *Merry fucking Christmas.*

CHAPTER 2
HARDY

"It's not every day you see a boob on a call," Mike says as he starts restocking supplies in the rig.

"You all good here?" I ask, making a circle with my hand, ignoring his comment. "I've already cleaned her out and sent the patient care report in. Hoping to make it home before bedtime so I can relieve the sitter."

"Are we not going to talk about that little exchange back there?"

"What's there to talk about?" I drag a hand along my jaw, hoping he'll just let it go.

"You totally had a moment with the patient. Bella and her boob."

"Jesus."

"That's totally becoming a thing. Bella and her boob. Has a great ring to it."

"Can you not?" Turning my back to him, I head toward the door as he runs over, clapping a hand to my back, stopping me.

"Look, man, you've been here for a little over a year now and we've gotten really close, even if I am a little miffed that they gave you the promotion to lieutenant over me."

I turn to look at him. "Fuck off." He teases me about this once a week. Mike is as unserious as they come.

He holds his hand up in protest. "You make a good point. Totally well-deserved, boss."

My brow lifts in response.

"Like I was saying. I've known you since you moved here and stole my promotion out from under me, and I've never seen you show any interest in a girl before. Never heard you mention a date, or a hookup. You don't talk about women, let alone flirt with anyone, and I get it, I know you're still getting over Lydie. But maybe it's time to get back out there. Do something for yourself for once."

I think over his words. Maybe he's right. "Lydie was one of a kind, and there's not a day that goes by since she passed that I don't miss her. And it's been really hard on Avery not having her mom around. But I'm not about to hop into bed with the first person that shows me her boob."

The thought of hooking up with Bella excites me, but I'm not going to parade women in and out of Avery's life. My little girl gets attached to things easily, and I don't want to break her heart again. Especially when I'm the reason her mom is gone.

"Just think about it. That's all I'm saying." He holds up his hands in defeat as he backs away, and I head to my truck to get home to my girl.

We moved to Chestnut Mountain about a year ago. I worked in a very active fire station in Denver, and I was practically living there with as much action as we saw. Moving here has been a nice break from the nonstop work calls and constant reminders of all the ways I let my family down.

Chestnut Mountain has been a much-needed change for us. Since the population here is under a thousand, most of the fire brigade double as EMTs depending on the type of call that comes in. When I started, I was desperate to prove myself and desperate for a distraction and was able to move up to lieutenant in just under a year. But that came at a cost

—I buried myself in as much work as I could, and before I realized it, Avery was closer to the nanny than she was to me.

It was eye-opening, and I decided to cut my hours and put her needs first. That first year after we lost Lydie was tough. It was hard to see through the fog of grief, and learning how to become the sole parent to a little girl wasn't easy. There was a lot of therapy, for both of us, and even though I've made lots of progress towards acceptance, I still struggle with the guilt.

I made a lot of mistakes over the past two years, and seeing how my actions directly affected my girl shook me. Therapy has helped Avery deal with her feelings, and our family sessions have brought the two of us closer.

But I'm not about to jeopardize the progress we've made by letting a potential hookup distract me. Even if she was stunningly beautiful and stirred something in me I haven't felt in years.

When I walk into the house it's late, and I shut the door quietly in case Avery's already asleep and drop my bag in the laundry room.

"I just put her down if you want to see her. She had a rough night," Maggie whispers as she comes up behind me. "I should have known better than to start on her homework after trick-or-treating. It took a while to get through it, and you're going to need to check it."

"It's kindergarten, what kind of shit are they giving her that could be difficult? I can email her teacher." That would be a good idea actually, since I've never met her and missed the fall parent-teacher conference because of an emergency call. It would probably be worth filling her teacher in on Avery's mom too.

"It's not that it's difficult," Maggie says, walking over to the coffee table to grab some papers. "It's that it was a family tree project."

Shit. Yeah, I definitely need to talk to her teacher.

"Avery helped me fill in what she could, but she shut down when we got to her mom's side of the tree."

I rub at the knot forming in my chest and look over the half-empty family tree. Hell, I don't want to fill it out either. This is going to take a glass of bourbon or two to get through, and I remind myself to follow up with my therapist about this.

"I was able to lift her spirits with leftover Halloween candy, but I might have overdone it because she asked for three books and still had the wiggles when I left her."

"Thanks, Maggie."

She nods as she heads toward the door. "See you tomorrow, Hardy."

I quickly empty my bag and a small hamper of clothes into the washing machine and start a load of laundry, and then I head up to see my little girl.

When we moved here, I let Avery go wild picking out any decor she wanted. I couldn't bring her mom back or take away her grief, but I wanted to make sure she had her dream room. We painted the walls light pink, with a bright pink accent wall and dozens of butterfly decals placed sporadically throughout the space.

"Hey, baby girl," I say, sitting on the edge of her twin bed.

"Daddy!" She scoots out from under the covers, climbing into my lap as she wraps her little arms around my neck. I inhale deeply, savoring the scent of her strawberry shampoo. "Miss Maggie let me have Tootsie Rolls!"

I smile against her hair. "I heard."

Avery's therapist mentioned working on improving open communication with her and validating emotions, and one of the things that has helped us the most is focusing on the positive, even if my default tends to be pessimism. It's hard in my line of work, when I often see people at their worst moments, but I try to be a steady and calming spot in their day. When I come home, though, it takes everything in me to keep up the happy when all I want to do is hide away from the world. But kids don't let you do that—they force you to be the better version of yourself, whether you want to or not.

"What's something that made you laugh at school today?"

"When it was story time, we sat on the rug and someone farted!" She delivers the news like it's the most amazing thing that's ever happened to her, and I can't help but laugh. "And no one would fess up. Everyone was laughing and pointing at someone else."

"That sounds like a fun day."

"Was your day fun?"

I think back to the beautifully awkward woman I met that I can't get out of my head. "It was a good day. Are you looking forward to Christmas now that Halloween is over?"

She lets out a deep sigh. "Not really. I wish I could move to the North Pole and live with Santa."

Shit, did I fuck things up that bad last year?

I have a million follow-up questions in my head, but it's late and sticking to her bedtime routine is important, so I tuck her in and kiss her goodnight, unsure of how to respond to her.

As I head to my room, my mind races with thoughts.

I wish I'd been around more to help Lydie with this stuff.

I should've paid more attention to all these traditions.

How can I fix this for Avery?

Is there anyone who could teach me how to be better at this?

Even though therapy has helped me process my grief and be the best version of myself for Avery, I still feel like I'm not doing enough. Do all parents feel this way?

I lie in the darkness and let my anxiety torture me until sleep takes over.

CHAPTER 3
BELLA

"Oh my God, it was so embarrassing! My tit was out the whole time!" I take a swig of my water and cringe as three sets of eyes narrow in on me.

"Like the whole thing? Are we talking heavy cleavage, or did it include areola and nipple?" Raven asks matter-of-factly. She's always been the pragmatic one of the group.

"The whole fucking titty," I answer, hanging my head.

"That's mortifying. I would be mortified. Were you mortified?" Summer asks.

I shoot her a what-do-you-think look.

"Hold on, I need more information to get a clear picture about what we're talking about. Why was it flopping out of your shirt? Where was your bra?" Raven asks.

"Umm, how about 'are you okay and why did you need an ambulance?'" Lucy asks.

"Clearly, she's okay. She's here." Raven points at me as if this is obvious.

"Not emotionally. She clearly needs to talk about it," Lucy says, placing a hand on my forearm.

"I do. And to answer your question, I was hooking up with

this guy and he'd already gotten my bra off and my shirt was low-cut, so when I passed out, gravity took over."

"You passed out?" Summer gasps.

"Yup. I've had some awkward hookups before, but this one wins the title for the worst. Between the passing out, almost tossing cookies in front of the hot EMT, and the accidental flashing, it was an eventful evening, and I didn't even get an orgasm out of it. Just a stupid bladder infection probably caused by my new birth control."

"But you're okay now?" Lucy asks, and I nod. "Okay good, now tell me more about the hot paramedic."

Summer keeps glancing at the door. "I don't mean to be that person, but we have, like, fifteen minutes before the rest of the moms get here for the PTO meeting, and you know that Amber is always early."

Shit, she's right. "Good point. So, I'm in the back of the ambulance and the EMT is super hot, and I had to ask him to put my tit back in my shirt."

"Can we stop saying 'tit'? It feels wrong saying it in a room where kindergartners hang out all day," Summer says as she shifts in the too small chair.

It's my turn to host the November Parent Teacher Organization meeting, and my classroom is where we're meeting tonight, despite the fact that there are other classrooms with adult-sized chairs.

I continue recapping the events. "So, he covered up my *breast* and then called me a *good girl*."

"Umm, that's kind of weird," Raven says.

"Oh shit, I forgot to say that between the redressing and the praising, he had to put an IV in and I started to panic. I swear he made bedroom eyes at me and then he *good-girled* me to calm me down."

Lucy leans back in her tiny chair. "That's hot."

"What are bedroom eyes?" Raven asks.

"You know, like this," I say, and then give her a seductive onceover.

"Never do that to me again," Raven says between laughs.

"What was his name? Tell me you got his name or his number." Lucy is practically bouncing out of her seat, leaning over the table as she speaks.

"He said his name was Hardy, no number. I've never seen him around town before," I reply.

"I think I sold him a house! Tall guy, dark hair, great jawline with the perfect amount of stubble? Lives in a small two-bedroom cottage on the side of Nicholas Bluff, on the edge of Chestnut Mountain limits?" Summer asks, rapid-fire.

"Sounds like his description," I confirm. "No clue where he lives, though."

The door swings open, and the air grows thick with Amber's heavy, sickly sweet perfume as her nasal voice interrupts our conversation.

"Oh good, you're all here. Are you going to just sit there gabbing, or are you actually going to help me set up the meeting?"

With my back to Amber, I roll my eyes to the group and slowly stand to help. In minutes, we have all the agendas dispersed among the tables as parents start arriving.

"It's a shame you didn't clean your room before this. What's the point of getting here early if you aren't going to prepare for the meeting and make your room look presentable?" she says, pointing to the bucket of crayons in the corner of the room that spilled in the chaos of dismissal earlier today. "Wouldn't want the town hearing about yet *another* mess you made."

I take a calming breath before I reply, choosing to let her dig roll off my back like water on a duck. As a boy mom, I'm the queen of letting shit go. "I'll allow it" is a frequent mantra of mine since sweating the small stuff only brought me ulcers and nervous bowels. "Eh, I figured I'd get to it when I get to it. This is a kindergarten classroom, after all. I don't think anyone's going to care about some spilled crayons." Just like no one should care about my messy private life since the divorce.

The responding twitch in her eye almost makes me laugh out loud. Instead I hold a fist to my mouth and fake a cough.

"Remind me not to put you in charge of Santa's Workshop," she mutters under her breath. "Don't need you screwing another thing up like you did your marriage."

I blink in shock. "What was that?"

Before she can answer, several parents walk in the room, and Amber gestures for me to go hand them the sign-in form before turning her back and effectively dismissing me.

As I trudge over to the door, Summer links her arm with mine, pulling me off course as she turns me to face her.

"About that guy you were telling us about…"

"Yeah?" I ask, my brows pinching in confusion.

"Don't look now, but he just walked in."

My head swivels toward the door, and I spot the tall EMT who recently touched my boob.

"I said don't look," Summer hisses, but it's too late. Hardy spots me, and he lifts a brow as his eyes roam down to my chest and back up again.

In a panic I look down at my chest, worried I'm exposing myself again. Nope, all covered. Phew. When I look up at him again, he's chuckling, and I cringe at my awkwardness.

This is why I do hookup apps. Get in, get off, get out, all before I can open my mouth and let my awkward turtle loose. That, and once guys learn I'm a single mom with a teenage son, my sexy meter drops to zero.

"Bella, the sign-ups!" Amber's nasal voice singsongs in that syrupy tone you use when you've told someone to do something three times now and they haven't done it but you don't want to come across as a bitch.

I start walking toward the door, almost in slow motion,

stopping in front of Hardy as I thrust the clipboard toward him, saying nothing.

He looks at me confused, before he takes it and pulls out a pen. "This is a blank sheet of paper. What am I writing on it?"

"Your number," I say, then quickly squeeze my eyes shut. Shit. Maybe if I keep them closed, he'll disappear.

He clears his throat, and I open my eyes. The corner of his mouth lifts. "Do I get your number if I give you mine?"

"I...uhhh. It's a sign-in form for the meeting. You put your name, number, and email."

"Ah." His piercing blue eyes scan my face before settling on my lips. "You didn't answer my question."

My eyes drop to his very naked ring finger. A throat clears behind him, and I see a line of parents forming. "Bella!" Amber's voice calls out.

"I'm just gonna..." I hook a thumb over my shoulder and then turn and walk over to my desk, wishing I could crawl under it. Why do I have to be so awkward with this man?

Minutes later, Amber calls the meeting to order and introduces me as the faculty representative. I also have a kid at our K-12 school, but I don't correct her. She moves meticulously through each agenda item, sneaking glances over the secretary's shoulder, probably to make sure she's taking sufficient notes.

When we get to the holiday section of the agenda, I watch as parents raise their hands to volunteer for parties, fundraisers, and other events.

"Unfortunately, the person organizing Santa's Workshop had to drop out and we need someone that can fill in at the last minute since it's only a month away," Amber says, looking around the room.

"I can!" My hand shoots up. It happens so instantly, I'm not even sure why I'm doing it.

You're doing it to prove to this grinch that you are not the total hot mess she thinks you are.

Amber plasters on a big fake smile, looking around for someone else to raise their hand, but no one does. "Actually, you'll need a co-chair."

"I'll do it," a deep voice says from the back, and I don't even have to look to know it's Hardy.

Three sets of eyes look at me, and I can hear their voices in my head.

Is that who I think it is?

Oh my God, you're right! He is so cute!

Why are you volunteering for that?

I bite my lips as I give them a small smile.

"I guess that will work." Amber's voice is strained as she continues. "What's your name, and who's your student?"

"I'm Hardy, and I have a kindergartener named Avery."

Oh shit. My eyes go wide, and I try to hide my surprise. How did I not know he had a kid in my class? Avery never did have a parent show up last month when we did parent-teacher conferences. And I've never had any trouble with her, so I haven't needed to call home.

I smile and nod through the rest of the meeting, not really paying attention as my mind races with thoughts.

How the fuck am I going to pull off Santa's Workshop?

Am I allowed to date a parent of a student in my class?

Would he even be interested?

The room has nearly cleared out by the time I refocus my thoughts.

Amber walks by my desk. "Let me know if you need any help with Santa's Workshop. This is a really important event. The kids look forward to it all year. I just want to make sure you know how big a deal this is."

I look at her and fake a smile. She comes off as a difficult person, but I know she means well—or at least I want to believe she does. But if her persistence comes from a place of caring, I wish she'd care a little less. "I know how important this event is. Christmas is my favorite holiday, I have tons of ideas for what we can do, and I won't screw this up."

"You better not." She turns on her heel and click-clacks out of the room.

Hardy is still sitting at his table, picking at the wrapper on his water bottle. It's clear the man doesn't skip leg day, because there's no other explanation for how he is holding up his body as he balances on the chair that looks comically tiny under him.

I stand from my desk and walk around the tables, picking up the leftover agendas, trying to straighten the place as much as I can while sneaking peeks at him out of the corner of my eye. He really is handsome, and I wonder if he noticed all the moms checking him out during the meeting. I know I did.

I turn my back to him, cleaning up the container of spilled crayons, silently cursing Amber with each one I pick up. I'm hyperfocused on my task, getting totally lost in the silence of the room as I sort the crayons by color.

"So, there's something I want to ask you about."

I jump. "Holy shit, I forgot you were here," I say, shooting up as I turn to face him.

He's still seated at the table, the wrapper of his bottle now fully removed as he twists it between his hands, his eyes locking with mine. "Sorry, I didn't mean to scare you."

"It's okay." My hands feel sweaty, and I wipe them on my pants as I approach his table. "Can I join you?" What is it about this man that makes me so nervous? "Sorry, I don't know why I asked that. It's my classroom, and you said you wanted to talk, of course I can join you."

The chair slides out in front of me completely on its own, and I look around in confusion. "Do you have elves under there doing your bidding?"

He chuckles. "It was my foot under the table."

Of course it was. Get it together, Bella.

"What's up?" I plop into the seat with as much grace as one of my students after recess.

"About the other night. Are you doing okay?"

Oh my God, are we going to talk about this now? I swallow nervously, unsure where he is going with this. "Totally fine. All better. Just a bad bladder infection because of my medication. All healed. We don't have to talk about any other part of that night."

My leg bounces under the table as his eyes sweep down to my chest. Is he flirting? This feels like flirting. Is he even single? This could get messy, and I'm so over Amber spreading more gossip about me around Chestnut Mountain. I need to remain professional, even if he is the most delicious man I've ever seen and I want to lick every inch of his body. I squeeze my thighs together and shake the thought from my head. "Let's talk about Avery," I say, changing the subject.

"Is Avery doing okay? In class, I mean."

"Avery's great. She's super helpful to all her classmates, very respectful in class, and follows directions. You all are doing a great job with her." *Smooth, Bella.*

He winces. Shit, what am I missing?

"My class size increased and I'm having a hard time keeping up, and clearly I didn't read her file thoroughly enough. I didn't even realize you were Avery's dad until you said it in the meeting. My life has been a hot mess lately. I'm so sorry. Is there something going on at home that I need to know about?"

"Mrs. Williams isn't in the picture."

"Oh! Got it. No worries. I'm divorced too. I totally get it."

This time he flinches at my words, and I feel like the biggest asshole on the planet.

"Not divorced."

I wait for him to say more. Note to self: Check Avery's file as soon as he leaves.

"So, you're worried about Avery because your wife left?"

He drops his head in his hands and blows out a long breath.

Oh, fuck.

She didn't leave them. Why am I the most awkward person in existence? Why can't I pick up on context clues and have a normal conversation? "I'm so sorry, Mr. Williams, my neurospicy brain sometimes doesn't pick up on social cues. Are you saying that Avery's mom died?"

His head is still in his hands as he nods. I'm not sure if he's crying, trying not to cry, or trying not to scream at my daftness.

"It's okay. Well, it's not, but it's going to be. How long ago did she pass?"

"It'll be two years in January," he says against his palms.

"Got it. Okay. If it makes you feel any better, I couldn't tell. Avery seems very well-adjusted, totally on grade-level with her peers. And I'm sorry I overlooked that in her file. That's something I would've noted to keep an eye on. Regardless, I think you're doing a great job with her." I place a hand on his arm, and a tingle zips through me at the connection.

He lifts his head, studying the place where we're connected, and I self-consciously pull my hand back, but he stops me, placing it back on his arm as he covers it with his palm.

"Thank you… for saying that."

"It's the truth." My words are husky, and I barely recognize my own voice.

"I need to confess something." He leans forward in the chair and my heartbeat quickens in my chest. His eyes drift down to my lips, briefly. It was quick, but I caught it. Does the hot EMT want to kiss me?

"You can tell me anything," I say breathily. What has gotten into me? I don't come on to my students' parents and I don't typically flirt with men like this, but something about this man has me desperate and needy.

"I fucked up Christmas last year."

The words are a bucket of ice, extinguishing the lust coursing through me.

"I'm sorry, what?" I blink away the fog.

"It was her first Christmas without her mom. And I fucked it up. Apparently, I didn't do any of the things that Lydie used to do and everything was ruined. I had no clue half of what she did. I was always out on emergency calls or at the station. She did all the magic shit."

"I'm sure that's not true."

"First, she was upset because Sprinkle McPinkle Pants never showed up."

I chuckle at the name. "Her elf?"

"Yeah! See, this is what I'm talking about. You just know. How the fuck was I supposed to know what that was? It took me a week to find where Lydie used to hide it and then I still didn't know what the hell I was supposed to do with it."

"Lemme guess, you had an upset little girl the next morning."

"How did you know that?"

"You didn't make the elf move."

"How the fuck is a doll supposed to move?" he asks, waving his hands in the air as he speaks. I miss his touch instantly.

"You don't make it move in front of her, but every night the elf is supposed to report back to Santa on its kid."

"So, it's like a creepy spy?"

"That's one way to look at it."

"Is there another way to look at it?"

"It's the magic of Santa! The elf reports back, and when it returns, it usually gets into mischief. And the kids wake up to see what shenanigans the elf got into."

"I have to let this stupid spy doll trash my house too?"

"There are whole websites dedicated to giving parents ideas about how to move their elves. I've seen some of them get pretty elaborate. Luckily my kid was never into all of that, but I will warn you that we usually do classroom elves, so you've got a few weeks before he shows up. That should give you enough time to figure out what to do with yours."

"I appreciate that," he says with a hint of snark.

"I'm happy to help if you want. I can print a list of ideas you can try."

"Anything would help. I can't ruin Christmas again."

"You say that like there's more to the story."

He lets out a deep sigh. "I burnt the cookies for Santa and forgot to get milk. I threw them away after she went to bed, and when I came downstairs in the morning, Avery was sobbing because her cookies were in the trash and she thought Santa put them there."

I slap a palm to my mouth to cover my laugh.

"I completely forgot about the stockings—"

"Why do men always forget about the stockings?" I say to the sky in jest like I'm speaking to myself, and I catch him smirk.

"I'll never make that mistake again. Avery was devastated. I may have mentioned that *I* forgot so now I'm worried she's going to think I do everything, not Santa."

"Not a problem."

He raises an eyebrow at me, but I offer no further explanation. "I know there's more I probably forgot that Lydie did. I'm not completely inept, but I worked a lot, practically living at my old station. I don't know how she did everything she did, she just took care of everything, and I guess I figured she'd always be around to do it."

"Moms make magic," I say, offering him a small smile as I place my hand on his, squeezing gently.

Our eyes drop to our hands as warmth spreads along my skin everywhere it touches his. I can tell by the way he shifts in his tiny seat that he feels it too.

"I just want to make sure that she has the perfect Christmas this year. I'm willing to do anything it takes, I just need some guidance in the right direction. We've been through so much and I know she misses her mom, and maybe if I can get this right, it'll be like she's still here with her." His voice breaks at the end, and I can tell he's trying not to cry, but I can see how misty his eyes are as he blinks rapidly. "I want her to believe in Santa. Maybe if she does, she'll stay my little girl for a little longer. She's had to grow up so much the past two years without her mom."

"It's not dumb, and it's okay if she doesn't believe in Santa. Lots of kids don't," I assure him.

"That's just it. She *does* believe in Santa. She just thinks Santa doesn't love her. I know it probably has something to do with her losing her mom and the misplaced feelings are now on Santa."

"I would be happy to help with that in any way I can."

"Would it be weird to ask you to ask her everything her mom did so I can know? Like, be discreet about it and talk about everyone's favorite traditions and then report back to me."

"I can absolutely do that, but I can also do one better. If you thought this PTO meeting was wild, you should come to the after-hours one."

He looks at me quizzically, cocking his eyebrow as he tilts his head.

"Sorry, I made the connection in my head, and I realize you didn't follow my train of thought. Some of the moms get together and have a private PTO meeting with booze. And for some odd reason, lots of dick jokes. But I'm sure they'll tone it down in mixed company. You should come."

He shifts in his seat, rubbing the back of his neck, and I can tell I'm losing him. "I don't know if that's my scene."

"Oh, it's your scene, trust me. It's full of moms, and we can fix this little problem of yours."

"How?"

"By teaching you The Santa Rules."

CHAPTER 4
HARDY

It's been a few days since the PTO meeting, and I'm packed into a circular booth with four moms. One of those moms is incredibly fucking hot. That same mom is also my kid's teacher and is off-limits. So tell me why I volunteered to help with Santa's Workshop? Clearly, my dick is the one calling the shots here.

Picking at the label on my beer, I try to focus on their conversation, but Bella was right. There are a *lot* of dick jokes. I want to join in, but part of me is worried about offending them, and I really need their help, so I refrain.

After a quick round of introductions— Lucy is the other blonde, Raven has black hair and a permanent scowl, and Summer is the brunette who keeps nervously looking around anytime someone in the group makes a too loud dick joke—I try to get the ladies to focus on the task at hand.

"I don't want to be a dick—"

"He said it, everyone drink!" Bella shouts, and the ladies all take a swig of their drinks.

"Are you gonna drink every time I say dick?" I ask.

"Yup," Lucy says as she downs another shot and the rest follow suit.

I blink at them, half-shocked and half-impressed. These women could keep up with most of the guys in my battalion.

"I think we broke him," Summer says as she waves a hand in front of my face.

Shaking my head, I look around the table. "Definitely not broken. I can assure you every part of me is in working order." I say the last part to Bella, nudging her leg under the table.

The flustered look on her face is adorable as she reaches for her cider and misses, knocking it over. Lucy swoops in to catch it before it spills. The move seems almost choreographed, like it's not the first time it's happened.

"So you don't need help with a certain appendage?" Lucy asks teasingly as she moves her eyes from my face to my crotch in rapid succession as Bella lifts her drink to her lips.

"Depends on who's offering." I look at Bella and smile when I see her comically large swallow. It has all sorts of dirty thoughts running through my head.

She doesn't acknowledge my comment, but her cheeks pinken as she fills them in on my problem, recapping how I royally fucked up Avery's first Christmas without her mom. I shift in my seat as they all take turns giving me sympathetic glances. The attention has my stomach in knots.

Bella beams as she turns to me. "Are you ready to learn the secret to Christmas that will change your life?"

"Okay, I think you're overselling it a little," Raven says.

"I think my life changed the night I showed up at your place on a 911 call. But sure, tell me your Christmas secrets."

Bella's mouth drops open and then snaps shut as the rest of the ladies swoon. I can tell I've distracted her, so I nudge her with my foot. Her thigh rubs against mine in the process, and I tamp down the urge to slide my palm under the table, grip her leg, and trail my hand higher until I can feel if she's damp in her panties.

Where are these thoughts coming from?

I pull my leg back from hers, shoving down the inappropriate thought. This woman is my child's teacher. And I'm going to be working closely with her over the next few weeks. Getting involved with her is probably not the best idea right now. I've got to get my libido under control.

But you haven't thought about another woman like this since Lydie.

If Bella notices my inner turmoil, she doesn't show it as she clears her throat, gathering our attention. "We treat Santa like a streaming service."

The women all nod like this is a revelation, and I cross my arms on my chest, waiting for more. "I'm not following."

"Santa is a subscription. You know how all these apps have different tiers you can subscribe to? That's how we treat Santa."

Summer quickly scans the room, then props her elbows on the table. "Your kid is young, so you might not have experienced this yet, but at some point, she'll find out that her friends got more or less from Santa than she did. I'll never forget the day that my kid came home and asked me why Santa brought his friend a PlayStation and all he got was a LEGO set. I was at a loss for what to tell him that wouldn't ruin the magic."

"The Santa Rules make it easy. There are different tiers. If Avery's friends brag about getting an iPad, all you do is explain that her friend's parents subscribe to a different tier, so that's why they got different gifts," Bella explains.

"It's an easy way for your kid to understand without you having to admit that you're broke," Raven adds. "This way, if her friends get more, they're on different tiers."

"What are all the tiers?" I ask, my mind already struggling to keep up with how complicated this must be.

A huge grin lights up Bella's face. "That's the best part. It's whatever you decide it is based on your traditions or preferences. Only want to have Santa bring one gift so you get credit for the rest? It's a tier. Want Santa to bring all the gifts? It's a tier. Want Santa to bring three gifts like the wise men? It's a tier. Want to teach your kids how to budget and have Santa bring under a certain dollar amount? It's a tier!"

"You get a tier, you get a tier, EVERYBODY GETS A TIER!" they all shout in unison as they clink their drinks and take another sip.

Lucy claps her hands excitedly. "Literally whatever you already do is a tier. It's a great way to honor everyone's unique traditions and cultures and explain it in a way kids can grasp."

"And you can opt in or out of anything. Live animals, clothing, large electronics, baby brothers, video games, weapons like Nerf guns, or anything else you can think of. Your kid wants a pet? Sorry, we opted out of live animals," Bella adds.

"In my house, we opt in to Santa's toy trade-in program—he picks up our old toys, and the kids get new ones. I tell them that we can donate our unused toys to Santa so he can fix them up and share them with others. That allowed me to shift the focus to helping others and giving back. Then I sneak the box of toys to donate into my trunk and drop it off at Goodwill," Lucy explains.

"Girl, you're a better person than me. If I did that, those toys would be in my trunk for months, outta sight, outta mind. And then one of my kids would find it later and Christmas would be ruined," Summer says with a laugh.

"Also, your little stocking problem is totally solvable," Bella says.

I shift in my seat. "I want it on record that my stocking isn't little."

The ladies take another sip of their drinks.

"Noted," Bella says as her eyes rake down my body. "Santa can help with your not so little stocking. Since you let it slip that you fill it, you can explain that you opted out of Santa-filled stockings. And then you can encourage her to shop for yours too."

Are there any problems moms can't solve? "I'm kind of in awe of you ladies right now. This is incredibly thought out and thorough."

They all smile, and I wrack my brain trying to think of anything I can to stump them. "What about that damn elf?"

Raven bangs a fist on the table. "I hate the fucking elves!"

Bella breaks into a fit of laughter, and the sound warms my chest. "You can opt out of elves, like anything else you don't want to do, but after what you told me about last year, I'm afraid that won't be an option for you."

"You're probably right," I grumble as another thought hits me. "What about all the mall Santas? How do you explain those?"

"I got this." Summer cracks her knuckles. "Mall Santas are Santa's helpers. Since he's so busy at the North Pole, he sends out helpers in his place so he can keep toy production on schedule. And his helpers collect wishes and lists for him and report back. It's an easy way to explain why all the Santas look different."

"You've really thought of everything," I say.

Lucy smiles understandingly. "I wanted to keep the magic alive with my kids but didn't want them to feel left out when their peers got more from Santa than they did. Not everyone can afford to go all out. If my kids ask Santa for something that is a hard no, I simply tell them we opted out of that service or that it's not included with our tier. I explained that I chose the smallest option because we didn't need much from Santa and wanted him to provide more to others who needed it or chose it."

"The emphasis is on giving and not receiving, then?" I ask. The innuendo is unintentional, but all four women burst into laughter.

"He's a keeper," Summer says on a laugh.

Wiping a tear from her eye, Lucy continues. "I never wanted my kids to feel unloved or less than because I couldn't afford to get them an Xbox. But I also didn't want to shame other parents from going all out with their Santa-giving, so I chose to word it in a way that emphasized that some parents choose to have Santa take care of everything for them."

Bella leans in, and her sweet mint scent permeates my nostrils as warmth spreads in my chest. "And if someone has a tradition that you don't, you can use the rules to explain it. For example, I used to hang wrapping paper in the entryway and Isaac would run through it on Christmas morning like a football player coming out of a locker room. It was a fun way to keep him from peeking under the tree while also building suspense."

"I remember you guys doing that!" Lucy says.

Bella's cheeks pinken. "Yeah, it was the source of a lot of fights. Despite the fact that we hung it every year, Jake acted like it was the first time every time and could never get the angle right."

Summer slaps her hands over her mouth trying to contain her laughter, and I chuckle.

"Don't say it!" Bella laughs.

"That's what she said." I say, and the table loses it. Everyone's laughing, but anger swirls in my gut at her comment about her ex. Why does that bother me? Am I jealous?

Once they regain their composure, I ask, "What else do The Santa Rules cover?"

"Was that not enough? We invented a set of rules to keep the magic of Santa alive. That's no small feat," Raven says matter-of-factly.

I hold up my hands in defeat. "You're right. This is awesome. Thank you."

"Ooh, a man who not only can easily admit when he's wrong, but says those magic words. Lock him down, Bella," Summer says as she jokingly fans herself, and my eyes flick to Bella's. Has she been talking about me to her friends? Is she into me? From how red her face is, I'm going to say yes.

Lucy leans in, pulling the focus off her friend. "Do you have a brother as handsome as you?"

"Sorry, just a sister."

The music shifts in the bar, the upbeat pop replaced with the opening notes of "Santa Baby" as Bella groans, downing the rest of her cider.

"Here it comes," Raven says.

"Gird your loins," Summer agrees.

I look around in confusion.

"I hate this song!" Bella exclaims.

"What's wrong with this song? I thought you loved all things Christmas?" I ask.

"I'm down for a little sexy Santa." Lucy waggles her eyebrows.

Bella lets out a sigh, her shoulders slowly relaxing. "A sexy Santa can get it. I'm all for a sexy bearded man who lets me sit on his lap."

My dick twitches at her words, and images of her bouncing on my lap flood my brain. Me thrusting up into her while she grinds her clit against me, her tits jiggling with every thrust. I blink several times, clearing the thought and looking at her, but she refuses to make eye contact with me as she continues.

"That's not the part that bothers me. It's the way the woman focuses on what Santa can do for her. I'm fine with an older man lavishing gifts on his woman. And if the song wasn't about Santa, I'd have no problem with it. It's the way it focuses on *me, me, me*. Give me this, buy me that. I deserve this, I want that. It is the antithesis of the spirit of Christmas. It focuses on what she gets and not the spirit of giving."

"Holy shit, you're totally right." Suddenly I feel like I know this woman on a deeper level, and I can't explain it. She's just talking about a song she hates, but the way she's describing it is so much more. Bella is thoughtful and cares deeply about others, and I want to know everything I can about her.

"Speaking of songs," Summer says, breaking the spell.

"Circling back to The Santa Rules, you can also use them to explain the creepy parts of that Santa song."

"Which one? There are a lot of songs that mention him." I throw back the rest of my beer.

"I can never remember the name of it, but you know the one about watching you when you're sleeping and awake, knowing if you're good or bad."

"Ah." I nod along as Summer continues.

"Kids grow up thinking Santa is some all-seeing omniscient presence in their lives. One year my kid decided he thought Santa was fake because how could he watch everyone all the time? Since we opted out of the elf, I told him the parents watch their kids and report back to Santa on the app, and that's how he decides who's good or naughty."

"That's genius. Wait, there's an app?" I ask.

Bella shakes her head. "There's not, we just tell the kids there is, but wouldn't it be cool if there was? It could list out all the tiers, and you could customize it so whatever you told your kid, it would show it in the app like the official tier. Kids could write letters to Santa directly in the app to save paper."

"Or they could do that if those mall Santas creep them out," Raven adds.

"Exactly!" Bella continues. "We could have a photo section with frames where you could add Santa to your pics. Have a map to link to certain charities, food kitchens, donation centers, Toys for Tots, and angel trees. Ooh, and links to cookie recipes, or online cookie contests directly in the app!"

"Of course, we would have to have a parent section with a passcode, so you could go in and change anything you wanted to, and your kid couldn't peek behind the curtain and have the magic ruined," Raven adds. I get the sense she is the most practical of the group.

"And a Santa tracker!" Lucy adds.

"Ooh, and a message board where parents can share all their elf ideas!" Summer says.

"You know some of these apps already exist, right? Like the photo one and the NORAD tracker," I say.

Their faces fall. Shit, I'm ruining another Christmas.

Bella places a hand on my arm. "Okay, Mr. Grinch. But in our app, they could all be in one place!"

Her optimism is infectious as the women continue bouncing around ideas. I let them speak for several minutes, not wanting to interrupt or bring down the vibe with my pessimism. I'm struck by Bella's spirit, how tenacious she is. I don't see her as the hot mess that she thinks she is; in fact, making her flustered seems to get me hard, just like that moment in the ambulance when I called her a good girl.

She's exactly what I need to help fix my Christmas problem. I'm not clueless—I know I could google shit and figure it out on my own, but the stakes to get this right for Avery feel unbearably high. And Bella seems to love the holiday.

I need to figure out a way to spend more time with her, to pick her brain about everything Christmas, to see what she can get Avery to tell her. I want my little girl to believe again; I want some part of her childhood to feel normal, but if I ask her to tell me everything and then I do it, she'll know it's me and not Santa making it happen. It's obvious I need help, someone to coach me through it, and listening to Bella share all the hoops she jumped through to make things special for her son post-divorce has convinced me that she's the perfect person for the job.

Once there's a lull in the conversation, I look around the group. "So, what I'm gathering is, pretty much anything you think of can become a Santa rule."

Bella's face lights up. "Now you get it!"

CHAPTER 5
BELLA

I flop into the chair in the principal's office the following Monday after school. "Are teachers allowed to date the parent of one of their students?"

"Well, that's a fine how-do-ya-do!" she says as she lowers her bifocals and peers at me across her desk in her sternest face.

"Sorry." I stand and act like someone is rewinding me as I walk backward to the door and try again. "Hello, Principal Adams. I would like to discuss a very important matter with you."

"Cut the crap. When have you ever referred to me that way?"

"Sorry, Aunt Delilah."

"That's better. Now what can I do for you?"

"Could I, in theory, date the parent of one of my students and keep my job?"

"There is no school rule against dating a parent. Honey, this town ain't big. Everyone's kid goes through this school at some point, and it'd be impossible for you to date anyone if that was a rule. And it'd be impossible to enforce."

"I'm sure Amber would help police it," I say, rolling my eyes.

"That busybody would report her own shadow to the neighborhood watch. Don't pay any mind to her. If you're treating all students equally and not showing any favoritism to your beau's child, we're good."

"I would never treat anyone any differently," I say. I may be a hot mess at times, but I love my students deeply, and I would never do anything to hurt any of them.

"I know you wouldn't. Just CYA as they say, cuz you know Amber's gonna come sniffing around. She's a handful as a parent, but she's gotten insufferable as PTO President. Thank goodness her son is so easygoing."

Nodding my head in agreement, I laugh. Amber's son is a grade behind Isaac and is the exact opposite of his mom.

"So, I have your blessing?"

"Not that you need it, but yes," Delilah says.

"Thank you! And don't worry. I'll keep it under wraps." I jump out of my chair and lean across the desk to hug her.

She laughs. "You'd think I just handed you a pack of condoms and told you to mount the man."

I shake my head. "Delilah, you can't talk that way at school."

"What? There are no kids around."

"I will never understand who gave you this job."

"No takesie-backsies!" she says to the ceiling as if there were cameras watching her.

I laugh, knowing this is just how she is. My mom and Delilah were best friends, and when my mom died at the tail end of high school, Delilah raised me well into adulthood. It's safe to say the perverted little apple didn't fall far from the family tree.

We know how to cut up, but when it's time to be serious, Delilah is as professional as they come. I, on the other hand, tend to vacillate between awkward weirdo and perverted weirdo, though my students get teacher weirdo. Delilah runs our school with the utmost care, but she's also a fun boss, and the teachers and kids love her.

"So, tell me all about this hot dad that you're willing to risk your job over."

"You said I wouldn't get fired."

"No, I just said there's no rules against it," she says with a wink.

I blow out a breath and opt for honesty. Chestnut Mountain is known for its gossip, and I'd rather her find out from me than the rumor mill. "His name is Hardy Williams. Avery is his daughter."

"Ah, the widower."

"Has everyone read her file but me?" I mutter out of the side of my mouth.

Delilah picks up a pen and grabs a sticky note. "Doesn't follow directions," she says slowly as she writes.

"What are you doing?"

"Nothing, just making a note for your permanent record," she says, ripping the note off the pad.

"You know those are made up, right? We just tell the kids they exist so they behave."

"Oh, they're as real as Santa." She places the sticky note on my face.

Ripping it off, I flip it over and read it. "This says, 'Get some' and then there's a doodle of a dick."

"Did you get some dick yet?"

"No, I've been talking to you this whole time."

"Like I said, doesn't follow directions. So, tell me more about the hot firefighter."

"I never said he was a firefighter."

"This is a small town, you don't think I'd notice when a hot new man moves to town and starts handling a big hose?"

"I'm gonna pretend like I didn't hear that. And technically

he's an EMT too," I say. "Great, now I can't get the image of him holding his firehose out of my head."

"You're welcome. Bella, you're still young and you have plenty of life ahead of you. Go hump the hot firefighter."

I laugh as I grab my bag and head for the door, and then I turn back to her. "Got any plans tonight?"

"Why, honey, the world's my oyster, and I'm gonna pop that puppy open with my sword!" Delilah says.

"I don't think that's how the saying goes, and nobody should be giving you a sword," I call over my shoulder as I head out of the office.

CHAPTER 6
HARDY

When I pick up Avery from school the next day, Bella waves us down in the carpool line.

"Hey! Do you wanna plan a time for us to get started on the PTO stuff?" she says, glancing at Avery.

I raise an eyebrow until it hits me that she's talking in code so Avery doesn't catch on.

"Sure, I have some time now. Will that work?"

"Oh? Oh! Yeah, sure. Isaac is at his dad's this afternoon so we could do it at my place."

"Sure, let me drop Avery at the house and have Maggie come over to watch her. What's your address?" I ask as I open the maps app on my phone and hand it to her.

She types it in. "I'll see you over there in a bit."

"Are you going to Miss Carlisle's house?" Avery asks from the back seat once we pull out of the parking lot. Avery doesn't quite have all her L sounds yet, so it comes out "Car-while" instead of "Carlisle."

"Yeah, we're working together on a special project for the school."

"I wanna help!" she whines.

"You would be bored, baby girl. We're going to be talking

about boring stuff and making lists. It's not gonna be fun," I assure her.

Twenty minutes later, I'm admiring all the inflatables decorating Bella's yard.

When she opens the door, there's a huge grin lighting up her face, and I can't help but smile back. I gesture at the inflatable of an upside-down Santa in a chimney kicking its feet. "I like what you've done with the place."

"That one's my favorite. I kinda have a thing for Santa, but I love a good stuck-in-the-chimney gag."

I scan the rest of the yard. "They're all Santa-themed."

"It wasn't intentional. I want to get other ones, but I'm on a budget and stick with whatever I can find for half price after Christmas." She steps back, ushering me inside.

"So, this is what the rest of your house looks like," I say, looking around her space. It's a cozy little house with simple furnishings yet has a modern feel. A small kitchen opens to the living room, giving it an open-concept design. There's an office and a half bathroom, and I know the bedrooms are upstairs since I was here on that call a little over a week ago.

"Shit, I totally forgot you've been here. That was super embarrassing, by the way."

"The guy that called it in, is he your boyfriend?" Super subtle.

"Who, Brenton? No, he was just a guy I met on DTF."

I swallow my surprise and start coughing immediately, feeling like I'm choking. She's on hookup apps?

"You okay there, big guy?"

Punching a fist against my chest, I exhale, finally. "Didn't take you for a hookup app kind of girl. Not that there's anything wrong with that."

"Chestnut Mountain is a small town, and people talk. And everyone here already knows all my business, so options are limited when it comes to dating."

My eyebrows pinch. "And how does a hookup app solve that?"

"Well, it's also a very popular tourist spot. They're in and out and don't get attached. And I mean that exactly how it sounds. In and out." She wiggles her eyebrows.

"Oh, I got it," I say, a twinge of jealousy hitting me. Why the fuck does the thought of her hooking up with other guys make me jealous?

"I haven't really dated since my divorce four years ago. Just random hookups when I'm in the mood. Plus, I know as soon as I put myself out there, this town will be talking all about it, and I'm not sure I'm ready for all that. It was hard enough dealing with all the rumors after my divorce."

I remind myself to ask her more about that later. "Is it okay for me to be here? I wouldn't want to start any rumors to slander your good name."

She swats a hand at me. "It's fine. Avery is my student, and we're working on a school project. If anyone says anything, we totally have an alibi. But if we'd gone down for coffee at Chestnut Roasters, there'd be rumors about us for days. It would probably be in the town newspaper. *Local, hot mess mom woos handsome firefighter.*"

I rub my jaw, trying to hide my chuckle at her antics. "That is not how the headline would read."

"What would it say then?" she asks, crossing her arms over her chest in challenge as she raises an eyebrow.

"*Grumpy firefighter annoys beautiful, young kindergarten teacher.*" I shrug.

Her responding laugh is a soft tinkle, like bells jingling on a sleigh. "I'm not sure my teenager would agree with your youthful assessment of me."

"I think my assessment is accurate. And I believe there was mention of a mom wooing me?"

She swallows, and I track the movement in the column of her throat. I really want to know if we're on the same page with where this could be headed, and I wait for her reply as I reach out and tuck a loose strand of hair behind her ear.

"You can't say things like that to me..."

I pull my hand back, feeling the sting of her words. "Sorry."

"I wasn't done. You can't say things like that to me because it makes me want to kiss you."

Neither of us move as her words hang between us, heavy like smoke that refuses to clear. "And you don't want me to kiss you?" My heart races as I wait for her answer.

Our eyes meet, and a bolt of something passes through me. Judging by the way my cock is responding to it, I think it's lust. I'd almost forgotten what it felt like to be genuinely attracted to someone. I've noticed a pretty girl here and there, but this is more than that. For the first time since Lydie, it's not just someone's looks that I find appealing, and the thought of that scares me a little. I don't deserve a second chance at love.

There's a clatter near the front door, and she steps back, turning toward the noise. "Isaac, is that you?"

"Who else would it be?" a squeaky teenage voice shoots back. "Are your tits covered?"

Her eyes flick to mine in apology as I slap a hand to my mouth to fight back a laugh. "I told you to stop using that as a greeting when you enter the house."

"How often are your tits out?" I ask, shooting her a smirk.

"Oh, sorry, I didn't know you had company," he says as he enters the room and then turns on his heel.

"Come back here. This is Hardy. He was the EMT who helped me the other night. His daughter is in my class, and he's helping me with Santa's Workshop. We were just talking about our plans."

Isaac walks over to where we're standing, dragging his feet as he moves. He looks over the papers spread out on the table, and his eyes light up. "That looks cool. Do you need any help?"

"I will never turn down help from you." She smiles as he takes a seat on the opposite end of the L-shaped couch.

"Hey, I'm Isaac." He gives me a nod.

"Nice to meet you."

"She teach you about The Santa Rules yet?"

Bella nods at me. "It's okay, he's in on the secret. He's a Santa now too."

"She did," I confirm.

"Cool," he says, in that way only a disinterested teenage boy could.

"Dad just drop you off?"

"Yeah, a few minutes ago."

She looks at me, hooking a thumb at Isaac. "It's like pulling teeth with this one."

"It's the opposite for me. Avery doesn't even need me in the room to have a full-on conversation. She's just like her mom." Her eyes soften, and I realize this is probably the most I've spoken about Lydie with someone since she died, besides Mike and my therapist.

"It snowed pretty good last night, huh?" Isaac asks.

And we've made it to the part of the conversation where we talk about the weather.

"Yeah, I'm really gonna have to talk to Mother Nature about only snowing when you're here. I had to shovel the driveway all by myself, and I am not built for that anymore," Bella says.

Isaac leans back on the couch, a shit-eating grin taking over his face, and I know this kid is up to something. It takes Bella a minute to catch on, but once she sees his face, she drops hers in her hands, pinching the bridge of her nose. "Isaac, how many penises are hidden in my yard right now?"

"I didn't draw any in the yard," he says, holding his hands up like he's innocent, but it's obvious from his tone that he's not telling the whole story.

"On my house?"

"None."

"On the windows?"

He shakes his head.

She lets out a deep breath before changing the subject. "How's your dad?"

"Good. He wants me to come out to his place for Christmas this year since they're renting a cabin in Aspen."

I can feel the anger radiating off Bella as her shoulders tense. "Do you want to go?" It's obvious there's more she wants to say, but she's holding it in.

"I dunno. It's like four hours away, and I wanna be closer to my friends."

"And it's my weekend," she mutters before slapping on a smile, her tone suddenly chipper. "Well, let me know what you decide. I would love to see you on Christmas, but if you want to see your dad too, I understand."

"Thanks, Mom. I'm gonna go log on. The guys are waiting for me," he says as he stands, and I watch him walk to the stairs.

Once he's out of earshot, I hear a muffled noise and turn to see Bella screaming into a pillow. "It's fine. This is fine," she says as she fluffs it and places it back on the couch.

"It's clearly not fine. Why didn't you say something?"

She leans her arms on her knees. "Isaac is thirteen. He's a year away from being able to choose if he wants to live with one of us full-time and I don't want to lose him."

"You have a custody agreement, right? I don't think the State of Colorado would allow that."

"We do have an agreement, but once a kid is fourteen, the courts take their opinion into consideration more. I doubt they would rule against him living with me, but I don't want to risk it. Jake can woo him with expensive gifts and vacations, and I can't compete with that. His family comes from money, and I'm barely making ends meet on a teacher's salary."

Suddenly, some of her Santa tiers make more sense.

"But what I lack in fancy gifts, I make up for in quality time. Well, as much of that as a teenager can handle. I want him to feel seen and loved when he's in my house since I know my ex doesn't spend a lot of time with him."

"Isaac can see through all that," I say, leaning forward so I can look in her eyes.

"You think so?"

"I do. I was a teenage boy once. He just needs to know that he's loved and safe. Plus, he's at that age where his friends mean more to him than anything else, so you might have that in your favor."

"Look at you, finding the bright side. Maybe I'm rubbing off on you."

I'd like to rub something on you.

"Hardy Williams, did you just make a dirty joke in your head?"

My jaw drops, a mix of shock and confusion on my face. "How did you—"

"Your face is beet red, but the tips of your ears get red too when you're really embarrassed or turned on."

Why does it make my dick hard that she notices that?

"We should really figure out a schedule for when we plan to get together to work on this."

"That's a good idea."

"And maybe..." I trail off, building the courage to ask for what I want.

Her eyes light up, bright and full of hope. "Maybe?"

"Maybe, you could help me with the Santa stuff too?"

"Like a private tutor?" she asks, wiggling her eyebrows again.

"A Christmas coach?" I offer.

"Oh, I love that! And you'll be my Santa student! My life may be a bit of a disaster, but if there's one thing I'm good at, it's teaching. And Christmas."

"We should probably exchange numbers, then?" My palms feel sweaty as I run them along my thighs.

"That was really smooth. Hardy's got some game."

"And we probably need to meet again, since we didn't get much accomplished for the workshop today."

She smiles, and my heart leaps in my chest at the thought of spending more time with this incredible woman.

———

BELLA

[picture of the hood of a car]

HARDY

What am I looking at?

Sorry, the snow kind of melted so it didn't hold its shape. It's supposed to be a penis

Why is there a penis on the hood of your car?

Isaac

I need more than that

That's what she said

When I asked him last night if there were penises in my yard, he said no

Clearly you didn't ask the right question

Clearly!

He drew a dick on your car?

Yup. I drove around town all day running errands in a cock car!

A wiener wagon?

A meat machine?

That sounds like a food truck

A jalopy Johnson!

Are we talking just the penis or were balls involved?

It was the whole unit

Then I think we should amend it to jalopy junk

You're right. That encompasses the cock and balls

It's decided

Thanks, I needed a laugh

Do you want to stop by my classroom tomorrow so we can keep talking about the workshop?

CHAPTER 7
HARDY

School just let out, and I'm waiting in Bella's room while she walks Avery down to the gym for after-school care. I'm finding it harder to resist this woman, but today we're focused on the mess we signed up for. Organizing Santa's Workshop.

I have no clue what I'm doing for our own holiday festivities let alone how to organize something so monumental for an entire school, but I'm willing to learn, and I'm certain I'm in the right hands with Bella. If anyone can help me save Christmas, it's her.

The sound of her heels in the hall warns me of her approach, and her face lights up when she sees me. She closes the door behind her as she pulls a chair up to her desk and motions for me to sit. Thankfully this chair is adult-sized because my quads were burning after sitting in the kid-sized ones for the whole PTO meeting.

She drops a stack of papers on her desk and looks at me with a mischievous grin.

"Before we get started here, something has been eating away at me and I have to ask."

Raising my eyebrows, my curiosity is piqued.

"Am I the only person who's exposed a tit to you on a call?"

My gaze shoots to her in surprise as I laugh. Her boldness is extremely sexy, and I can't help but be taken aback by her question. "I can honestly say I've never seen someone's tit fall out during a call before."

There's an adorable look of triumph on her face.

"I have been flashed intentionally, though."

"Stop it, you have not."

"Yup, apparently you're not the only one that thinks I'm hot." I cringe as soon as the words come out of my mouth. What am I doing?

"You know, that should embarrass me, but it does not." She folds her arms under her chest, propping her tits up on them.

My eyes rake down, drawn to her cleavage before traveling up to her lips. They're full and so fucking kissable. Holy shit, do I want to kiss them.

"So, what's Santa's Workshop?" I ask, averting my gaze, breaking the tension, as I tug on the back of my neck.

She looks at me with a blank stare, blinking slowly. I'm not sure if she's uncomfortable because of the way I was checking her out, or if she's teasing me about my question. "I mean, I know it's where Santa works at the North Pole, but in the context of the school, and whatever it is I volunteered for, what are we talking about? We didn't really get to that part the other night."

"Are you telling me that you signed up to help run this and you don't even know what it is?"

"Well, the lady running it is really hot, and she's already showed me one of her boobs, so I was kinda hoping she'd show me the other."

Her head falls back in laughter, and my eyes track the delicate column of her throat, wishing I could grab it while driving my cock into her. *Tamp it down, man.* Clearly this woman has awoken something in me that I'm having trouble containing.

"Santa's Workshop is a fundraiser the PTO does every year. Where most of the fundraisers we do aim to raise money for the school, this one raises money to give back to families in need in the community. Basically, we buy cheap items, mark up the price by a dollar or two, sell them, then donate the proceeds. The kids come through and do all their holiday shopping for their families. Parents usually send cash in an envelope that has names of who they're shopping for and a budget for each person."

I run my hand through my stubble as I survey the papers on her desk. "So, what are we looking at here?"

"Amber dropped off a stack of papers from the chair of last year's workshop, but I swear that woman is determined to watch me fail. She is meticulous about her meetings and notes and has a color-coded notebook for everything, yet she hands me a disorganized pile of chaos?"

"That is weird." I pick up several sheets of paper that look like an itemized list of inventory, complete with sales prices, cost of goods, and potential profits. "This looks like the list of items they sold last year. I'll go through the stack and pull out any other pages that look like this. Do we have items left over from last year? Or do we have to buy inventory to sell?"

"I think there are some boxes of leftover items from last year in the PTO storage closet. We can go down there and look at what we're working with."

It takes us twenty minutes to go through all the papers and organize them into piles based on the type of document. Then she's leading me down the hall, toward the front office. I stare at her perfectly round ass the entire time as she gives me flirty glances over her shoulder. Most of the staff has already left, but I can still hear the faint squeaks of sneakers on the gym floor.

When Bella opens the door to the PTO closet, I'm assaulted by the chaos. "Holy shit, there's so much crap in here. Is there an organizational system?" I ask, looking around at the shelves full of boxes, only a handful of which are labeled.

"Apparently, Amber's organization only extends to her binders," Bella grumbles.

We decide to divide and conquer, each of us taking our place on opposite ends of the small space as we start at the bottom shelf and work our way up and over, pulling out each box to examine its contents. I'm starting to feel hopeless when we meet in the middle and are still coming up empty.

"I think it's those boxes on the top shelves. I vaguely remember a few of us shoving shit in here last year during the cleanup." She points to several boxes tucked in the back top corner of the room.

Backing up to get out of her way, she brushes against me as she walks over to the shelf. The move feels intentional, and my cock stiffens in response. I watch as she reaches up, exposing a sliver of her stomach. "Are you just going to stand there, or are you going to help me?" Her tone is flirty as she wiggles her ass.

"Go ahead. I'm just enjoying the view," I say, leaning against a shelf as I watch her stretch onto her toes, struggling to reach the top shelf.

She places a foot on a bin on the bottom shelf, trying to extend her reach, but slips. I lean over to catch her, wrapping an arm around her waist as I pull her into me.

My heart races wildly in my chest as our eyes meet, and I search her face for answers. Does she want this? Her eyes rake down to my lips, and she leans into me. I can feel the way her chest expands with every breath, and I close the distance between us.

There's an explosion in my chest the second her lips touch mine as the last of my resolve leaves my body and she moans into my mouth. I pull back to take a breath, and she reaches a hand up to my jaw, pulling my lips back to hers as I groan. She takes full advantage and pushes her tongue against mine. The taste of winter mint floods my senses, and I chase the flavor as I lick and suck while her other hand clasps my neck, pulling me closer.

Not an inch of space is left between our bodies, and I know she can feel the effect she has on me everywhere, my heart beating rapidly in my chest, each stuttered breath and ragged inhale, every moan that rumbles in my throat, and the bulge rapidly growing in my pants.

Just when I think I can't take another minute of this without being inside of her, she pulls away and steps back, untangling herself from me. The gravity of the situation hits me, where we are, what we're supposed to be doing. We're in the storage closet of a school making out like teenagers. My kid's school. And Bella is her teacher. But fuck, I like the way she feels under my fingertips.

Her hand rubs against her bottom lip as she stares at me, and I have trouble deciphering her expression. "Ummm…"

Ummm? That was the best fucking kiss of my life, and all I get is an ummm?

She must see the annoyance on my face, and she holds her hands up like she doesn't want me to come any closer.

"Was it that bad? I'm kinda out of practice," I say, scratching my neck, my nerves getting the better of me.

"Are you kidding me? Your tongue was doing more tricks than a poodle at the National Dog show. I felt like an amateur trying to keep up."

"You liked it?"

"A little too much." She waves a hand in front of her crotch, and my eyebrows shoot up. "I'm going to need a minute before we go back out there."

"Are you telling me you're wet? That you're standing in a storage closet dripping for me?" My voice is low, hungry.

"And he's a dirty talker. What are you trying to do to me?" She says the last part like she's talking to an imaginary being in the sky.

I take a step closer to her and grab her still-outstretched hands, pulling her flush with me again.

"Fuck it," she says. She grabs my cheeks and kisses me hard. Desperately. Like I'm the last cookie on Santa's plate and she hasn't eaten in days.

When I feel her grind her pelvis against me, I push her back against the shelving unit, holding the back of her head so she doesn't bump it against the hard wood. She hikes a leg up on my hip, and I grip it as I run a hand down her other thigh, encouraging her to climb me. And she does, like a tree, wrapping her legs so tight around my waist that I can't help but grind my cock against her center.

"That's it, use me. Make a mess in those panties," I say as I kiss down the side of her neck.

She arches her back, pushing her pussy against me as she rocks back and forth against me.

The door handle jiggles, and we pull back, looking at each other in panic.

"Is someone in there?" a nasally voice calls out. "I forgot my key."

"Amber," Bella whispers.

I set her down and readjust myself as I take in the flush of her cheeks, her swollen lips, the small mark I made on her neck. Shit.

"Coming!" Bella calls out as she retucks her shirt and smooths a hand through her hair.

"The door automatically locks behind us, so you have to have a key to get in," she explains as she moves to open it.

Amber walks in, pushing past Bella as though she knows exactly what she wants. I take a step back against the wall in the cramped space to allow her to pass. She grabs a box and walks out, stopping at the door briefly with her back to us. She turns her head slightly. "If this is how you two are going to run Santa's Workshop, I'll find someone else to take over."

I can see the anger flash in Bella's eyes. "Maybe we

wouldn't have to spend so much time in a closet if the PTO president wasn't setting us up to fail. Boxes aren't labeled, inventory is missing, and that joke of a stack of paperwork is atrocious. My seventh-grade boy has better organizational skills."

A laugh bursts out of me because I know how unorganized teenage boys are.

Amber's face doesn't move as she speaks in a fake-as-fuck tone. "I'm sure you'll figure it out." And then she leaves as the door slams shut behind her.

"What the fuck is her problem?"

"I hooked up with her husband in high school."

"Oh shit."

"It wasn't serious, and they weren't together then or anything. But a while back, we were at the bar after a PTO meeting, and he got drunk and started talking to me rather loudly about how he wished she was like me in bed."

"The fuck?" I clench my hands into fists.

"The fucked-up part was Jake, my ex, thought it was funny and started comparing notes. That was the beginning of the end of my marriage. It became clear I was more of an object than a person to him. Luckily, I don't have to see Jake much, but Chuck is constantly popping up at the school or the bar. Anyway, Amber hasn't liked me since, and we don't invite her to the after-hours PTO meetings anymore."

I have no words as the anger courses through me, the need to protect this precious woman strong. In the short time I've known her, I've seen how she cares for those around her and gives back to her community, and I can't imagine anyone seeing her for anything less than she is. Incredible.

"What do we need to do to make this the best Santa's Workshop ever?"

She laughs, and there's a twinkle in her light blue eyes. "Now we're talking."

CHAPTER 8
BELLA

An hour later, we're out of the storage closet and I'm following behind Hardy's truck to his place. Calm your tits—I know things were hot and heavy in the closet, but his kid is going to be there, plus mine is sitting shotgun grumbling the whole drive. And after that interaction with Amber in the closet, my need to prove myself to her is overriding my libido. Barely. The man is *hot*.

As we approach his adorable cottage, surrounded by the most breathtaking view I've ever seen, I'm reminded of two things. One, I love living in Colorado. And two, I really need to talk to Summer —the house she sold me looks like a shack compared to this.

Hardy slams the door to his truck and runs around to help Avery out of her booster seat. He picks her up, and she squishes his cheeks in her hands. "Can we have pizza for dinner?" Her eyes widen as she sees me trailing up behind him. "And Miss Carlisle can stay for dinner!"

I look at Hardy for confirmation. "It's fine with me," I offer.

"I'm in as long as there's pepperoni," Isaac adds.

"Great, it's a date." He grimaces. "Not like that, like a dinner date."

"Is Miss Carlisle your girlfriend?"

The look of panic on his face is comical.

"Yeah, Mom, is he your boyfriend?"

"Oh jeez, there's two of them." I roll my eyes attempting to deflect, hoping Hardy will hop in.

Isaac crosses his arms, and Avery looks at him and mimics the gesture, putting on her sternest pout. It's actually adorable, and I fight the urge to laugh.

I look between the two kids. "Hardy and I are working on a project for school. And we are happy to stay for a pizza *night*, is what your dad meant." Though I'd love an actual date with this man.

Avery's eyes light up. "Can I help? I love projects!"

Hardy looks panicked, and my heart softens. The love he has for Avery is evident on his face, and his worries about ruining Christmas echo in my head. I can see how much this means to him.

Since I want to be able to plan parts of it without little ears present—in case we talk about Santa—I opt for honesty. "There's part of this project you can help with, but there are other parts that are super boring with lots of math and paper-work. Which one do you want to help with?"

"Not the math."

"Good thinking. How about you show Isaac around, and the two of you can hang out while your dad and I do the math part? Then we can eat and work on the fun stuff after."

"Can we use glitter?"

"Maybe!" I don't want to commit to glitter yet—that shit gets everywhere—but I know already from class how much Avery loves it.

She runs up the steps to the house, and Isaac gives me an annoyed look over his shoulder as he trails behind her.

"I feel like I just watched a magician at work. How the hell did you get her to go along with that?" Hardy asks once we're alone.

"It helps if you give them a choice. I work with young kids every day. Now, teenagers are another story. Any advice on raising a teenage boy?"

"Make him do his own laundry."

I give him a questioning look.

"Just trust me on that one." He makes a motion with his hand like he's jacking something off, and I erupt in laughter.

"Oh God. Oh God! Gross. Do you think he's doing that already?"

"How old is he?"

"Thirteen."

Hardy laughs. "Yeah, he's doing it already."

I cover my mouth with my hand. "I'm gonna be sick, but that would explain why we're going through so much lotion and hot water."

"Mom!"

I shoot Hardy a did-he-just-hear-us look and turn to my son. My sweet angel baby son who I will absolutely not picture doing unthinkable things to his body. Not that masturbation is wrong, but it's just not what you ever want to think about in the context of your child.

My body shudders involuntarily.

"Hello! Did you not hear a word I said?"

Hardy jumps in before I can look at him.

"Sorry, she just got some disheartening news, she just needs a minute," he says with a small chuckle he cannot contain.

"Whatever. Grown-ups are weird."

I tamp down the nausea and let out a deep breath. "What is it?"

"They have an Alienware computer. Is it okay if I get on?"

It's not clear if he's asking me or Hardy, and we look at each other and shrug.

"You're not playing those shooter games," I warn.

"Actually, Avery and I are going to code a game from

scratch. I thought it'd be cool and would keep her occupied if you two are going to…"

He starts to trail off, and I jump in, interrupting him. "Work on a project."

"Is that what old people are calling it these days?"

I look at Hardy and offer him an apologetic smile, but he just stuffs his hands in his pockets, enjoying the show.

"I'm just messing with you, Mom. I was going to say I could keep her occupied if you two were going to talk about S-A-N-T-A stuff."

"That makes more sense. Yup. That would be great. Thank you, Isaac."

Once the kids are set up on the computer upstairs, Hardy clears a space at the kitchen table, and we get to work.

I pull out my newly organized binder and start flipping through pages.

"What made you come up with The Santa Rules?" Hardy asks, breaking the silence.

"My ex was never good at communication, and we weren't on the same page about a lot of things—still aren't. It kinda started as a way to cover for his lies about Santa. He could never keep things straight. And I wanted Isaac to believe. So I would explain it away as a new Santa Rule."

"And he bought it?"

"For a while. He was ten when he asked if I was Santa."

"What did you tell him?"

"That Santa isn't your parents. It isn't any one person. It's an idea, a belief in something more. It's joy and hope. And love. It's karma and believing in the greater good. It's doing things for others because you want to and not out of obligation. And I think that's important for kids to learn. Once they find out the truth about Santa, they get to become a Santa, and then they're part of keeping the magic alive for other kids."

We're fifteen minutes from our pizza delivery when an idea hits me.

"What if we ask for donations of used toys and home goods? That way we don't have to spend any money on inventory since Amber's budget is laughable. We could always say it's part of Santa's giveback toy refurbishment program."

"The Santa Rules," he says knowingly.

"Exactly! Then people can double donate, so even those that don't have money can donate items. And instead of keeping the leftovers, we can have a designated time for the kids whose parents didn't send in money to shop. Then everyone can participate. People can clear out their closets and their wallets!"

"That's actually a really good idea."

"And if any of the kids ask where the toys came from, we use The Santa Rules and tell them that they were donated by kids like them and Santa's elves fixed them up and brought them to us so we could help others. Then it encourages those kids to donate this year for next year."

"It could be self-sustaining that way," he says.

"Precisely!"

"I could put a box at the fire station to collect donations," Hardy offers, his eyes dancing with excitement.

"That would work better. One at the school might make kids suspicious. I can reach out to some local businesses too."

"Okay, this is a good start. I'm feeling better about everything. Now we just need to plan the layout of the room," Hardy says.

I scribble down some reminders in my notebook just as Avery bursts into the room.

"Is the pizza here?"

"Almost," Hardy assures her, holding up the app to show her the tracker.

"Can I help with your project now?" Avery asks as she hops on a chair and leans onto the kitchen table as Isaac takes a seat across from her looking only mildly uninterested.

"Sure!" I say as I collect the papers, worried about sticky

kid fingers making a mess on them that Amber will give me a hard time about later. "Your dad and I are helping put together a Christmas shop for the school. It's like a little pop-up store where students can buy gifts for their family and friends and we wrap them so they can take them home and put them under the tree. But we call it Santa's Workshop, even though it isn't the real workshop."

"Because that one is at the North Pole," she says.

I nod. "That's right."

Avery picks up a rough sketch I made of the workshop, holding it up to examine it closely. "What's this?"

I grab the paper and shove it in my pile. "Oh, that's just a really bad drawing of what I thought it could look like, but we don't have time to decorate it like that."

"We have to decorate it. It has to look like Santa's real workshop," Avery says. "Daddy can build it. He's good at that stuff. Can't you, Daddy?"

Hardy sticks a hand out, motioning for me to hand over the paper, and I reluctantly do. "I'm not an artist or anything, it was just a draft of a sketch."

"Are these zigzags trees?" he asks with the hint of a smile.

"They're supposed to be."

"Do you already have a Santa chair, or would that need to be built?"

"Wait, do you think we could actually build something like this?" I ask as I look at him in astonishment. What can't this man do?

"Oh, I know I could. It doesn't look too complicated. I could build some theatre flats or paint over existing ones if the school has some already. And I could cut some simple pine trees out of plywood."

"And we could wrap empty boxes to look like presents!" Avery squeals.

"Maybe the Chestnut Mountain Market would let us borrow their Santa chair? They usually have a Santa helper come out every year to take pictures with the kids since the nearest mall is over an hour away," I say.

"Then this should be easy. I could probably knock it out in a weekend," Hardy says.

"And we'll save a ton of money in the budget if we do what we talked about earlier, so we might be able to spend some money on supplies," I mumble to myself as I look through my notes to see if there's anything I'm overlooking that I might have committed to a budget.

"Please, Daddy!" Avery begs as she tugs on his sleeve bouncing excitedly in her chair.

Hardy turns to me and comically bats his eyes. "Please, Bella?"

If I thought telling his daughter no was hard, this is damn near impossible especially when he licks his lips and sticks the lower one out a little further making me want to bite it.

There's no way I'm going to say no, not to either of those faces. And not when I know how important this is to both of them.

"Okay! We're going to build Santa's Workshop!"

CHAPTER 9
BELLA

"Mom! MOOOOMMM!"

I come tearing down the stairs running toward his voice. "Isaac? Where are you?"

"In here! You have to see this!"

Turning the corner, I come face-to-face with my thirteen-year-old who, in the past few days, has magically eclipsed me by at least an inch in height. "What is it?" I ask, clutching my chest, willing my heart to stop racing. "With the way you were yelling, I thought it was an emergency."

He steps back, ushering me into the bathroom by grabbing my shoulders and moving me directly in front of the toilet.

The putrid smell assaults my nostrils first. But it's what I see when I look down that has me nearly about to dry heave. "Oh my God. Oh God. Is that your turd?"

I *am* going to throw up.

When I turn away—because how the fuck can I look at that baby arm trying to claw its way out of the toilet?—I gape at him in wonder. How did this skinny little body make *that*?

"It was a one-wiper," he says proudly.

I am done. Done with the conversation. But against my

better judgement, I continue to engage him. "What the hell are you talking about?"

"You know. A one-wiper. It's when you only have to wipe once and the toilet paper is clean. Isn't it funny how it takes two wipes to know it's a one-wipe turd, but it takes one wipe to know you're going to go through a whole roll just to get clean? I hate those ones when it feels like you're wiping a marker."

I stare at him dumbfounded, clamping my mouth shut so no more of this stench gets inside. "Are you seriously referencing *Parks and Rec* right now?"

"It's a classic. Wipe, a little bit of poop. Another wipe, still a little bit of poop. Wipe again, a little bit more poop. You keep wiping and wiping like you're swiping at a marker. *You know.*"

I speak out of the side of my mouth so I can't taste the smell of his bowels still permeating the bathroom. "I wish I didn't know what you were talking about. But I do *know* that Santa will not step foot in this house if you keep making smells like that. Now move. I'm not going to continue standing in this outhouse that you're trapping me in and listen to you give a dissertation on wiping your ass."

"I bet Dad would think it's cool. I mean, the head *is* poking out of the water."

I push my way past him, into the hall, moving into the kitchen with him hot on my heels. I turn around and pull him into a hug.

"You know, you have this annoying way of calling me an asshole, and I'm not sure I like it."

"Wasn't trying to," he says, trying to hide his emotions, but I can hear it in his tone and feel it in the single hitch of breath he lets out.

We stand there for several seconds as he lets me hug him. I can't remember the last time this kid let me hug him this long, but I can guarantee he wasn't almost my height, and his little body was a lot squishier and not so gangly.

"I don't want to go to Dad's for Christmas," he mumbles as he pulls out of the hug and stalks over to the cupboard.

"Oh?" I try to play it cool, but inside my heart is dancing like that meme of Oscar from *The Office*.

"Yeah. I mean, Aspen sounds cool, but I kinda wanna stick around here."

I deflate a little, realizing he's probably just wanting to hang out with his friends.

"I'm working on this gift for Avery," he admits quietly.

"You are? What is it?"

"It's a surprise." He shoves a handful of pretzels in his mouth, and I know he's done sharing, and I watch him saunter up the stairs to his room. When I walk by the bathroom, I look in and notice his turd poking out of the water.

"You didn't flush!" I scream after him, and he nearly falls down the stairs, grabbing the banister as he slides on his socks and darts into the bathroom to flush it.

"Sorry, my friends are waiting for me, and I'm AFK right now."

I don't understand half of the shit that comes out of his mouth lately, but when I look over at the toilet, I see the water slowly rising and realize it's clogged right as the doorbell rings.

Fuck my life.

"Come in!"

"Bella? We're still meeting today, right?"

"Hardy! I forgot you were coming. Don't come in here!"

His large body fills the doorframe, and I turn to look at him, plunger in my hand, ready to attack the beast.

"Holy shit, what is that smell?" he asks.

"It wasn't me. I need you to know it wasn't me. I mean, I know everyone poops and poop smells, but these odors didn't come from my body. Actually, that's not true. They came from the human that came from my body, so I guess in a round-about way, they did come from my body."

"I'm an EMT and a firefighter, Bella. Shit doesn't scare me. A turd on fire wouldn't scare me."

He peeks over my shoulder and glimpses the shit monster, and his eyes go wide.

"Okay, that thing is fucking scary. That came out of Isaac?"

I nod, trying to hold my breath so I don't have to inhale the fumes.

"Gimme that. I'll take care of this. Why don't you get set up with the Santa stuff?"

Blowing out the breath I was literally holding, I don't give him a chance to change his mind as I thrust the plunger at him and head to the kitchen to wash my hands, proud of the fact that I let someone help me instead of insisting I could do everything myself. Even when I was married, hyper-independence was my go-to coping mechanism. It got me through the grief of losing my mom, and it was a hard habit to break.

After he washes his hands, we settle in at the kitchen table.

"I've come up with a detailed list of all the things we'll need to do to collect the donations, inventory and price items, all the way down to when we can get into the gym to set everything up. Since Thanksgiving is next week, it doesn't give us a lot of time to find volunteers to help with setup, take down, wrapping gifts, and running the shop. Once we get back from Thanksgiving, we'll have about a week and a half to get everything done. But I think we can do it," I say. I can feel the small line forming between my brows as the stress of all this overwhelms me. But I'm going to prove that I'm not the fuckup Amber thinks I am. She may not believe in me, but I do.

"The guys at the firehouse can help," Hardy offers.

The look on his face is so earnest, so sincere that it takes my breath away as it hits me. For the first time in my life, I want someone's help. And not just that, I want *his* help. The way he's been showing up for me and Isaac makes me believe that he is someone we can count on.

"That would be great!" I nod as I flip through the papers, making calculations in my head. "This could totally work."

"What about the other thing?" he asks timidly.

"Are we still talking about you needing to see Righty? I can whip them both out now if you ask nicely."

"Jesus." He drops his head in his hands. "I can't believe I'm not going to take advantage of that, but I was talking about the private coaching for the Santa stuff."

"I know, but it's more fun to fuck with you. I actually have a list planned out for that too, and it all starts with the tree. You've put one up already, right?"

His blank stare is almost comical.

"Hardy Williams. This is unacceptable. I'm going to need you to stay after class and receive your punishment."

The way his eyebrows jump, nearly meeting his hairline, is almost better than the flush on the tips of his ears. I love getting a reaction out of this man. After hearing his heart-breaking confession the other night, I'm determined to bring him as much laughter as I can. Plus, it's hilariously sexy watching this man try to hide the bulge in his pants. That trouser snake is not small, and I mentally pat myself on the back every time I see him adjust himself.

"Seriously, though, Hardy, you need a tree. Preferably a real one, and you better hurry because the good ones get snatched up before Thanksgiving."

"I am not putting a live tree in my house. That's a fire hazard."

"That's fair. What about a fake one? You can get one that's pre-lit, so you don't have to fool with all the lights."

"Yeah, that sounds like a good idea. We had one like that, but the lights burned out and it was too close to Christmas to get another one. It was another thing I ruined last year."

"But you tried, and that's what matters. Avery sees that."

He offers me a small smile, scratching the back of his neck. I notice he does this when he feels self-conscious.

"What's the ornament situation?"

"Uh, we have them?"

"Is that a question?"

"No, we definitely have them," he insists.

"Do you have any traditions with them? Special ones? Sentimental ones? Do you make new ones to add to the tree? Does Santa bring you new ones and hide them?"

I've lost him. The look on his face tells me that not only does he have no idea what I'm talking about, but I've overwhelmed him with things he's never considered.

"It's okay. I'll come to your place on Saturday and we'll get everything sorted. Your job is to buy a tree before then and gather all the ornaments you have. I'll do some recon with Avery to see what she remembers. Sound like a plan?"

He nods, the relief on his face evident. "Thank you."

CHAPTER 10
HARDY

I've got the tree all set up when Bella arrives on Saturday. I'm glad I did a trial run because she never mentioned buying a tree stand, and I realized once I got the tree out of the box that I had no way to stand it up. The whole ordeal made me feel like shit—if I'd been around more for Lydie and Avery, I would have known this. It also makes me feel like I was a shitty husband, but I'm determined to be better, be more present. For Avery. And maybe also for Bella.

Everything is laid out and ready for Bella's approval, but unease gnaws at my gut. Something about this feels the tiniest bit wrong. The ornaments in the boxes are full of memories of Lydie. I can't help feeling like I'm somehow betraying her, allowing another woman in on this experience, something she and Avery used to bond over. What if it upsets Avery? What if Bella takes one look at the amount of Lydie in that box of ornaments and bolts?

Fuck. I really fucking like this woman.

The doorbell rings, and Avery bounds down the stairs to the door and throws it open without a glance.

"Avery Elizabeth Williams!" I bellow.

Her little blonde head pops out from behind the open door.

"You do not open the door without looking first."

"Yes, Daddy!"

"It's fine, it's just me," Bella pants. She's juggling several boxes, and a large tote bag is hanging from her arm.

I rush over and grab the boxes from her as she follows me into the kitchen and drops her bag on the table. "Sorry, we've been working on stranger danger safety drills. Clearly, I need to go over the one on answering the door again."

"What's that?" Avery asks as she climbs onto the chair and starts going through the tote. Bella gives me a reassuring glance, and I take a calming breath. My nerves are already frayed, and the woman just got here.

"I have all sorts of arts and crafts so we can make our own ornaments. This is the kind of stuff I live for."

"How much did you spend on all this?" I ask, looking over everything. For a woman who refers to herself as a hot mess, it sure seems like she has her shit together. I'll be damned if I make her pay for all this on her own, though.

"Practically nothing. I'm like a squirrel gathering up nuts throughout the year to store for winter. Everything here came from my craft closet, but the glitter came from my classroom."

Avery's eyes light up, and she hops off the chair, jumping up and down. "Glitter!"

"Your dad and I need to make some ornaments for our school project, and I figured you could make some too."

I give her a quizzical look, not remembering this being on our Santa's Workshop checklist, when she winks at me, and I get this is the cover story so Avery doesn't know about my Santa lessons. Warmth spreads in my chest at the realization of the lengths this woman is willing to go through to help my little girl and keep my secret.

"What kind of ornaments are we gonna make?" Avery asks as the door swings open, and Isaac appears, holding a smaller box in his hands.

"Isaac!" Avery squeals as she runs up to greet him,

attempting to hug him around the box. He lifts it up then sets his arms behind her head, still holding the box, as he gives her a quick hug.

"Hey, Butterfly," Isaac says.

Avery laughs and crosses her arms. "I told you I'm not a butterfly."

"I thought you liked butterflies?" he teases.

"No, I don't."

"But you have them all over your room," I interject, confused. She insisted we get them when we were decorating.

"Because they're pink and purple."

"Well, I think they're adorable just like you," I say.

"Butterflies aren't adorable. They're just sticks with wings," Avery says.

"Okay, Butterfly," Isaac says as we all gather around the table, unpacking the supplies.

"Avery, have you made your Santa list yet?" Bella asks as Avery's eyes flick to mine, and she shakes her head.

"I was thinking, we could turn our lists into ornaments and kill two birds with one stone. That way we can send the paper list to Santa and keep the ornament list on the tree, and when you're an adult you can look at it and remember what you asked for all those years ago."

Where does she come up with this stuff? I never would've thought of something so simple and creative, yet sentimental. Is this something all moms are good at or just her?

"Do I have to show you my list?" Avery asks nervously. "I don't want Daddy to see it."

If she's already thinking that way, I've fucked this up more than I realized.

Bella's eyes connect with mine briefly, and I can't tell what she's thinking. "How about this? You and Isaac go upstairs and work on your lists, put one in a letter for Santa, and make a smaller one for the ornament. Isaac will make his own too. And he'll help you write it in your best handwriting and then you can seal the envelope for Santa, and we can fold up your smaller version and glue it into this ornament," she says, holding out a clear round ornament. "Then you can fill this one up with as much glitter as you want."

"Yeah!" she squeals. She grabs Isaac's hand, pulling him upstairs.

As soon as they're out of sight, Bella's hands grab the collar of my shirt, and she tugs my lips to hers. I'm overwhelmed by the taste of peppermint as she licks her way into my mouth. Her lips are so soft and she tastes so sweet as she threads her hands into my hair, yanking at the strands. A needy moan involuntarily escapes me.

"He likes his hair pulled. Note to self," she mumbles against my lips, and then she's kissing along my jaw and my neck.

"How long do you think we have?" I growl as she focuses on a spot just below my ear that has my cock growing impossibly hard.

"Fifteen minutes tops," she pants between kisses. I pick her up and set her on the table, then push her legs open with my hips, trailing kisses down her neck now that she's at eye level. "Oh yes, that feels so good. Fuck, you have a wicked tongue."

That's not nearly enough time for all the things I want to do to this woman.

I slip a hand under the hem of her shirt as she writhes against me, grinding her jean-covered pussy against my cock. She leans back onto her elbows as I slide the boxes of art supplies out of the way, leaning over her as I rub my hard length against her. Propping up on my right arm, I glide my hand up her torso and use my thumb to pull down the cup of her bra until I can feel her hard nipple.

Her head falls back, and she bites her bottom lip to stifle a moan as I continue pinching her nipple and dry humping her like a teenager.

"O Holy Night, right there," she whimpers as I keep my pace steady while increasing the pressure on her nipple.

That familiar tingle starts to build at the base of my spine when suddenly Bella throws her arms around my neck, pulling me flush with her as she arches against me. My release hits shortly after, and we pant heavy breaths against each other's mouths as we come down from the high.

"Holy shit," she whispers against my cheek. "I haven't dry humped someone like that since high school."

I restrain the growl I want to emit at her words. I don't want to think about her doing that back then, and I don't want her doing that with anyone but me now.

"I should probably go change before they come back down here."

Her eyes roam down to my cock still half hard in my pants.

"Did I just make you come in your pants?" she asks incredulously.

I tug on my neck. "I can't believe my answer to that is yes."

"Why? That's hot as fuck. Thinking about you all horned up for me, wanting me so bad, but all you can do is rub up on me till you paint the inside of your pants. Fuck, I like that more than I should."

I bark out a laugh. The shit that comes out of this woman's mouth is never what I expect, and yet it always excites me.

"Though it's worth pointing out that you still haven't done a proper comparison of the ladies yet," she says with a cheeky grin.

"I figured I'd seen Lefty, so Righty needed a little love. But I'd love to give them both a proper greeting when there are no children in the house." Did I just refer to her boobs with the ridiculous names she uses for them? I'm so fucked.

An hour later, I'm cleaned up, the ornaments are made, and we're gathered around the tree hanging them with a bossy Avery guiding our every move.

"No, Daddy, that one doesn't go there." She puts her hands on her hips.

Isaac leans down. "Want a boost, Butterfly? Or are you gonna flutter up there and put it on yourself?"

She nods, and he picks her up, setting her on his shoulders as I hand her the ornament, and she places it on the tree.

"That's perfect. But where's the topper, Daddy?"

I look at Bella in a panic. "It's probably still in the attic."

"Not to worry, I brought options. Since it's a new tree, you need a new topper. Are you an angel girly or a star girly?"

"Which one has more glitter?" Avery asks.

"Ooh, good call, let's go with the star." She returns a second later with a gold star covered in glitter and hands it to Avery.

Still on Isaac's shoulders, she places the star on the tree. The four of us stand back to admire our handiwork, and I've gotta admit, it's a fucking awesome tree.

Isaac sets Avery down as I start grabbing empty ornament boxes to shove back in the attic.

"Avery, Isaac, can you two go clean up the supplies on the kitchen table?" Bella asks.

They go easily to the kitchen, and we stare at each other dumbfounded.

"What just happened?" she asks.

"I have no idea. She always whines about cleaning up."

"Isaac too."

Our eyes meet, and a subtle pink blush creeps into her cheeks. "Thank you for indulging me today," she says, and I smile at the innuendo in her words. "I know it sounds crazy to be putting a tree up before you've even had turkey, but we have a long list of tasks to accomplish and not enough time to do it in."

"I had fun," I say, raising an eyebrow, wanting to make sure she knows I mean our time in the kitchen was fun too.

"We'll get out of your hair," she says, swinging her arms nervously. Does she regret what we did earlier?

"I thought we established that I really fucking like it when you have your hands in my hair."

"That's right. Hair pulling is your kink." She takes a step closer to me, our bodies inches apart, yet she feels unreachable since a kid could walk back in at any moment.

"The next thing on our list better come with a babysitter."

"Why's that?" she says with a smirk.

"Because I intend to figure out your kink. You know, so we're even."

CHAPTER 11
BELLA

I'd planned to take Hardy caroling for the next item on our checklist, but when he mentioned exploring kinks, I knew I had just the thing.

He shows up at my place the day after Black Friday with an arm full of grocery bags.

"Ooh, a man who follows directions and shows up with treats. Yes, please."

He chuckles as I take the bags from his arms and start laying out the snacks. "You've been doing so much. I wanted to contribute. What's the plan?"

I hand him a bag full of tissue paper. "Open it."

He looks at me confused, but I brush it off, moving around my small kitchen to make us hot chocolates.

"Just consider it an early Christmas gift."

Like a clown pulling on handkerchiefs, he removes dozens of tissues before getting to the box at the bottom of the bag, pulling out the portable projector with a list of movies taped to it. "What's this?"

"That is for you and Avery. All you need is a white sheet or wall, and you can set up the projector and have a holiday movie night. I made a list of some of Isaac's favorites when he was her age."

"This is…" he trails off and swallows thickly. "I can't accept this."

"It's fine. I found it on a lightning deal online."

"At least let me pay you for it."

"You got snacks. We can call it even." I cross my arms, making it clear I'm not backing down.

"Thank you," he relents.

"You're welcome. When I asked the class what their favorite holiday movie was earlier this week, Avery didn't have an answer. I wasn't sure if you all used to watch any with her, but you two are embarking on this journey together and you get to make new Christmas traditions."

"I may need help setting this up. Do you think Isaac would do it? He's a lot handier at this tech stuff than I am."

"Sure, I don't think he'd mind. He's at a friend's, though," I say, placing a hand on his forearm. "But tonight, you and I are having an adult movie night."

"We're watching porn?"

I burst out laughing. "Oh shit, I didn't mean it like that. I just meant grown-up, kid-free, not porn. Why, is that a kink of yours too?" I ask curiously.

He walks to the couch, taking a seat as he threads his arms behind his head, making me squirm with how long he's taking to answer me. "I'm open to exploring our options."

"Well, shit, I was just gonna put on *Die Hard*, but this is even better."

He looks at me confused.

"You know, cuz it's a Christmas movie for grown-ups that you wouldn't watch around kids."

Then he says the only thing that could kill my lady boner for him.

"*Die Hard* isn't a Christmas movie."

"You know, I was going to put it on and let it play in the

background while you finally compare Lefty and Righty, but never mind. *Not a Christmas movie?*"

He tugs on his neck. "Shit, I'm fucking this up."

My mouth snaps shut, the fight leaves my body at his words, remembering the broken man afraid of fucking up Christmas. I cross to the couch and sit next to him, setting our hot chocolate on the table. "You're not fucking this up. You're just wrong about *Die Hard*."

"How am I wrong? Just because it takes place during Christmas doesn't mean it's a Christmas movie."

"Then how are we defining a Christmas movie? What does it have to have in order to qualify?"

His eyes light up as he thinks about his answer. "It's gotta have certain items that make it Christmas."

"This should be good, because I guarantee whatever you're about to say is going to either prove my point, or rule out a lot of other traditional holiday movies, thereby also proving my point," I say, crossing my arms.

"Okay, it needs to have a tree," he says.

"There are plenty of holiday movies that don't have a tree, so that's vetoed. Plus, there are multiple trees in *Die Hard*."

"Shit." He taps his chin. "Okay, I got it. It needs decorations, and Santa. If it has all of those things, it would qualify. And I'm not trying to rule out other films as holiday movies, I'm just trying to negate the merits of *Die Hard* being one."

"Have you even watched *Die Hard?*"

He crosses his arms. "I've watched it."

"Then you should know that it takes place at a Christmas Eve party at Nakatomi Plaza, and the party includes various Christmas decorations, including a large tree. John McClane even wears a Santa hat. *And* he sends the body of a terrorist down an elevator wearing a Santa hat and writes 'Ho ho ho' on his shirt. Not technically Santa, but I'm counting it. Check, check, and check." I cross my arms over my chest, mirroring him.

"I said Santa, and that's just two hats."

"So, you wanna play it that way?" I crack my knuckles. "Here's a list of movies off the top of my head that don't have Santa but are traditionally thought of as Christmas movies: *Scrooged, White Christmas, How the Grinch Stole Christmas, Love Actually, It's a Wonderful Life, Krampus,* and *Home Alone.*"

"There's no fucking way all that's accurate. *White Christmas* and *Grinch* have Christmas in the title, and *It's a Wonderful Life* is a well-established classic. I'd hardly call *Krampus* a classic. I've never seen *Scrooged,* and I think there's a similar debate about *Home Alone* being a holiday movie."

"Never seen *Scrooged*? Besides *Christmas Vacation* and *Elf,* it's in the top three for me."

He shrugs. "I was always out on calls or at the station."

"Don't you guys watch TV in your downtime?"

"I liked to read so I could be alone. The TV room at the firehouse was always full of people."

"Hardy, we have to remedy this. But not tonight, because I actually want you to watch *Scrooged.*"

"Are we not going to watch *Die Hard*?"

"I wasn't planning on it. I figured we'd start it and see what happens from there, but I gotta be honest, this whole conversation has shaken me to my core." I try to stifle a laugh. "I'm not sure I can continue this tryst. It's a shame because I was really looking forward to you meeting Righty." I place a palm to my chest in mock astonishment.

He grabs my hand and pulls me against him, lying back on the couch as I balance on his broad chest. His other hand slides up and holds my cheek as he pulls my mouth to his. Fuck John McClane, I want to yippee-ki-yay this mother fucker. Or would that make him the mother fucker, since I'm the mother in this scenario?

"Whatcha thinking about?" he says as he comes up for air. I blink down at him. "Fine, it's a Christmas movie. Now stop overthinking and kiss me."

His hands are everywhere, groping my ass, my hips, my back. My senses are on overload as his scent surrounds me. Pine, bergamot, and something smoky.

Our movements are frenzied as we hurry to undress each other. I tug his shirt over his head while he slides his hands up my torso, forcing me to lift my arms as he removes my shirt.

I sit up and make a show out of slowly undoing my bra, letting the straps fall off my shoulders as my hair cascades around my face. His cock hardens beneath me and he pushes it against me, growing impatient. He sits up, gripping my waist as his thumbs trace circles on my stomach.

Holding my bra up with one hand, I push him onto his back with the other as I rub against his erection.

"Fuck, Bella. What are you doing to me?"

"Making you work for it."

"Tell me what I can do."

"You can be a good boy and beg for me."

"I want it. Need to be inside of you so fucking bad. Need to feel how wet you are for me. Want to feel you squeezing around me. Want to see how you look when you come. And I swear to God, if you don't let me see those perfect fucking breasts, I'm going to lose my mind."

His hips continue thrusting underneath me as I slide my hand under the cups of my bra, covering my breasts with my arm as I hold the bra up with my free hand. "But you didn't say the one word I wanted most."

"Please. I will do anything you want. I have never wanted anything more in my goddamn life."

"So obedient." I toss the bra down next to me, nearly knocking over one of the cups of hot chocolate on the table. "Shit." I lean over with fumbling hands and catch the mug before it makes a mess. "Well, that wasn't quite the sexy reveal I was going for." I laugh, trying to cover Righty with the mug.

Hardy dips his pointer finger in the hot chocolate, coating it in whipped cream, then swipes it on my exposed nipple. I lower the cup slightly, revealing myself fully, and he repeats the gesture on the other side, before he takes the cup from my hands and sets it on the table.

And then he feasts like a man starved. Look, I enjoy some good nipple play as much as the next girl, but holy fuck, the things this man can do with his tongue. First, it's soft as it licks gently, lapping up the cream, and then he stiffens the tip and pushes it harder against my flesh. I'm foaming at the mouth by the time he pulls a nipple between his lips. Then he's sucking, and nipping, and flicking, oh my! And when he's satisfied that he's cleaned Lefty, he addresses Righty.

"Nice to meet you," he whispers against my flesh.

"Oh my God, did you just introduce yourself to my boob?" My head falls back in laughter, and I can feel the vibrations from his chuckle against my skin.

"I just wanted Righty to know that I appreciate her as much as her sister. Don't need her developing a complex since I don't see her as often."

Fuck, I think I'm in love with this man. He gets me. My heart, my humor, my dirty jokes. But I don't have much time to dwell on that thought before he is lavishing my nipple with attention.

"Oh God, yes, right there. Keep doing whatever you're doing with that magic tongue," I whine as my hips buck against him. My orgasm hits quickly and unexpectedly and I cry out, threading my hands through his hair, holding him against my breast.

"I love how you sound when you come. When we don't have to be quiet and sneak around. But I won't be satisfied until you're screaming out my name."

He reaches down and unbuttons my jeans, and because I'm awkward as hell, I do a clumsy downward dog move over him as he struggles to take them off.

"Panties off, now." There's a desperate yet commanding

edge to his tone, and I climb off him to shimmy them down as he kicks off his pants and boxers.

My eyes go straight to the giant candy cane between his legs. You know the ones I'm talking about? The ones they sell at the drug store that are comically huge and you think, "There's no way someone can eat all that." That's Hardy's cock: a giant candy cane that I'm desperate to taste. Never one to back down from a challenge, I slide my hands up his legs and lower my head between his thighs as I lick from the base of his shaft to his tip.

"You don't have to do that... Holy shit," he whimpers. That's right, this man fucking whimpers like no one has ever done this to him before. "I don't... I can't..."

My head pops up as I wait for him to open his eyes.

"Why did you stop?"

"What do you mean you *can't*? Seems like you can to me."

His eyes shift back and forth, his nerves as worn as a fire-pole after too many people have slid down it.

"I can't..." He pinches his eyes shut, and the tips of his ears turn pink.

Kneeling between his thighs, I sit on my heels and wait as he covers his face, speaking through his hands, his voice muffled.

"I've never come from oral. My..." he trails off.

I pull one of his hands away and tilt my head at him. "I get that this isn't the sexiest time to bring up a past partner. And maybe something's wrong with me if I'm hoping you're saying what I think you're saying, but... what are you saying?"

"No one has ever had any success completing the task. Most just give up, and Lydie wasn't really into returning the favor down there."

"Wait, wait, wait. Are you saying that you would go out to eat and *she'd* never return the favor? No slobbing on the nob? No teasing the tonsils with that big ole sausage?"

Did this man come from Santa's Workshop just for me? Guess I've been a really good girl after all, because he's too good to be true. I've felt what that tongue could do in my mouth and on my nipple. I can't imagine how it's going to feel when he makes a meal out of me.

"Jesus Christ, this is humiliating," he says as he drags a hand down his face. "She tried a couple of times, but I don't know if it was lack of skills, or if I was too big and her mouth was too small, or if we just weren't compatible that way, but I never finished from that. Maybe it's something I'm just not meant for."

"Well, I have a big fucking mouth, and I'm not one to back down from a challenge," I tease as I pull the ponytail holder off my wrist, secure my hair, and then settle between his thighs.

"Don't be offended if I can't…"

"Do not finish that sentence. You can and you will."

I look up at him. He's holding his breath like he's nervous, and I smile at him, raking my fingernails along his thighs, hoping to ease his nerves. "I'm just going to need you to do one thing for me."

"Anything."

"Be vocal. Tell me what feels good, if you want me to do a motion again, move to a different spot, go harder, softer, tug, pull, suck. Tell me." I look him straight in the eyes before I deliver the knockout punch. "And I love it when you moan loudly."

I lower my head to the tip of his dick, whisper a quick, "nice to meet you," and revel in his responding chuckle. And then I swirl my tongue around the crown, alternating between licking and lightly sucking, spending some time getting it wet as I add in a hand to jack him between mouthfuls. And with a dick like this, the activity lives up to its title. It's a fucking *job*, and I've never worked harder.

He bucks and moans under me, flexing his hips up to meet

me each time I attempt to take him to the back of my throat. "Attempt" being the key word, because I'm not sure it's possible to deepthroat this monster.

"Holy fuck. Yes. Oh, fuck yes. I like that." His voice is a needy whimper.

Gripping him by the base, I take just the tip into my mouth and swirl my tongue in a circle.

"I don't know what you're doing, but that, more of that," he moans.

I spit onto the head and use my other hand to spread the saliva down his shaft, still gripping him with the other hand. I suck the tip into my mouth while jacking him. Then, instead of swirling my tongue, I flick the tip back and forth, rubbing both sides of my tongue against his slit.

"Shit, shit, keep doing that. Feels so good. Just like that. Oh fuck, I'm gonna come. Holy shit. I'm going t—" He doesn't even get to finish that thought before he's exploding in my mouth, letting out a guttural moan as I slide down, taking as much of him as I can. I take my time licking and cleaning his shaft, reveling in the little sighs and gasps he's making.

When I pop off his cock, I wipe the corners of my mouth with my finger. Cuz I'm a lady.

His eyes rake down my body and a hungry look takes over his features while I laugh.

"Lie back and let me see what kind of mess you made while sucking my cock like a pro."

"Aww, you liked it?" I tease.

"Baby, you sucked my soul out of my goddamn body. Now I want to see if I can eat your soul out of your pussy."

The nickname makes my heart skip a beat in my chest, but I can't resist the urge to poke the bear. "Never came from head, but dirty talks like a sailor."

"I never said I was inexperienced anywhere else, just in receiving. I can give like a pro."

My back hits the cushion and he grabs me by the thighs,

lifting me off the couch as he brings my pussy to his mouth. Holy hot damn. The tongue on this man should come with a warning. *May experience mind-numbing pleasure.*

There's nothing to grab on to as I dangle from his mouth and grip the cushion under me, arching and bucking against him. Each lick lights up hundreds of nerve endings. When he wraps an arm around my hips, tugging my body against his, and pulls my clit into his mouth, I swear my vision blacks out. There is nothing on my mind but the feel of his tongue as it dances against my clit like an eager ballerina in their first performance of *The Nutcracker.*

"Yes, Hardy, oh fuck. I'm—Oh God—I'm gonna—" An embarrassingly loud, porny moan escapes me as my orgasm builds hard and fast, feeling like nothing I've ever felt before. Oh shit, am I going to…

My pussy flutters and pulses as the urge to let go is too strong to hold back, and when I look up at him, I notice an obscene amount of liquid covering his face.

"Did I just…"

"Hell fucking yeah, you did," he says in awe.

"I've never…" I've never come so hard I've not been able to finish a thought.

"No one's ever made you squirt before?"

I shake my head and throw an arm over my eyes as he carefully lowers me to the couch.

"I think tonight's lessons were productive," I rasp as he lies down next to me, wrapping his arms around me.

"We got a lot accomplished," he agrees.

It's nearly impossible to catch my breath, but I do my best as I press my cheek against his chest. His heart is beating rapidly, and I smile, knowing I have that effect on him.

"Wanna watch *Die Hard*?" I ask, looking up at him.

"I'd love to," he says, then we pull on our clothes and he reaches for the remote before snuggling against me. "Oh, I forgot to tell you earlier, the donation boxes are all set up at the station, and we've already had a bunch of drop-offs."

"That's great! Raven works at the local paper, and she's going to run an ad for us free of charge for a few days." I look over my shoulder at him.

"That should help. I should finish constructing the workshop by the end of next week, and then I can paint it a couple days after that."

"You really didn't have to do all that. It was just a bunch of tables in the library last year." I arch back to hold his cheek, willing him to see the sincerity in my face.

He shrugs like it's no big deal. "I couldn't say no to Avery. I know how important this is to you… and the kids. And I wanted to make it special… for everyone." He keeps trailing off like he's changing his mind about admitting more, and I smile like an idiot about it for the rest of the night.

CHAPTER 12
HARDY

BELLA

I've got a whole week of festivities planned
for you, so I hope you're ready!

I smile as I read Bella's text. She's used at least a dozen
emojis, and not all of them are Christmas or winter related.
Some of them look suspect, and I get nervous as I try to deci-
pher them.

Wait. Are the emojis the activities we're
doing?

Ding ding ding

I'm having trouble figuring out what they
all mean

Guess

Do I have to?

Such a grinch. It's more fun that way!

I shake my head, but I can't stop grinning. In just a month, this woman has become a huge part of my life, and I need to spend more time with her once the holidays are over. Would she keep seeing me? Do I want that? Would Avery be okay with it? Guilt picks at my brain, and I shove it away as I try to figure out her plans for the week.

So, ice-skating? Building a snowman?

Yup. Yup.

I skip over the ones in the middle, focusing on the obvious ones.

Shopping and wrapping gifts?

[gif of Cousin Eddie from Christmas Vacation saying "Bingo."]

What is that third one? I know the next two

It's ginger

Gingerbread house!

See, this is fun, isn't it?

It'd be easier if you just told me

[gif of the grinch smiling.]

Are we visiting Santa?

Maybe?

That's vague

My hope is that Santa will be coming

Is that a chestnut?

It is

Please tell me we aren't roasting them over an OPEN FIRE? You do remember I'm a firefighter

Actually, it was code for something else…

That's one activity

I stare at the string of emojis for several minutes trying to figure out its meaning. But I come up empty.

Okay finger pointing at sparkly nuts?

OMG

BWAHAHAHAHAHAHAHAHAHA

That's even better than what I had planned!

What did you have planned?

Let's just say there's a certain adult activity that I would enjoy doing with you

Are you saying you want to ride this cock until I nut in you?

Fuck, I love it when you talk dirty to me

You kinda did the work for me on that one

Not to change the subject, because I could talk about what I want to do to you all day, but you know what tomorrow is, right?

THE SANTA RULES

December 1?

It's that magical day that Sprinkle McPinkle Pants returns

FML

No worries. Where did you hide it last year?

It's in my closet, tucked in an old pair of running shoes

Gross. You might need to air him out

You're probably right

Actually, this might work. We could do a scene that leans into the stink

As long as it doesn't involve Isaac's poop. I've seen enough of that to last a lifetime

Amen to that

I'm going to send you some ideas

Do you have a can of air freshener?

I think so

Do you have a printer and some tape? What about some treats? Usually when the elf returns, they have a note, and they bring treats

Why are there so many fucking rules?

I'm not the one who invented it! And I'm with you on the anti-elf stance. The only reason I do it in my classroom is because it's not worth the drama to skip it

I hate this

Want to come over tomorrow and I can show you some tricks? It might be good to plan out some elf scenes, so we don't double up

I can stop by your classroom after school tomorrow

That works, that's safe. We won't be tempted to strip each other down at the school. As long as we stay away from the PTO closet, we'll be good.

Okay. I can have Isaac hang out with Avery in after-school care and we'll make an elf plan!

Could I borrow Isaac today?

Sure!

Don't you want to know what for?

Nah. I'm sure it's above board. I trust you

I'm going to do the movie night for Avery

He'd love to help you get everything ready. But you need to pick up movie snacks. And supplies so you can do the elf tonight. Actually, I can send the leftover snacks from our movie night. We didn't eat much

I seem to remember differently. I'm pretty sure you had your mouth full that night

You know, you're right. And you did make a meal out of my cunt. We should definitely do that again

Wait, is that what the Santa emoji was before the others? You want to do that in a Santa suit?

I was waiting for you to catch on to that.

But I'll be naked, you'll be in the Santa suit

Jesus

An hour later there's a knock on my door and when I open it, Isaac is peering back at me, his arms full of bags as he stands on my porch alone. "Where's your mom?"

"She dropped me off, said she had to run an errand. Something about finding a Santa suit. I don't know."

I usher him in the house, and he hands me a note.

Hardy,

Isaac will help you set up everything you need to make this special. Put the projector in the living room and put all the blankets and pillows you have on the floor. Make it feel like a giant bed. And let her eat her snacks in there too. I know you're a stickler for eating at the table, but let her make a mess, even if it makes your eye twitch. (Then toss the blankets in the wash.) I promise you she will remember this for years to come. Also, there's a separate bag for the elf with instructions in it, and I included several ideas you can use this week in case we run out of time to plan. I'll be back in an hour to grab Isaac.

Bella

I look up at Isaac, but he's already emptied out the bags onto the table and pulled out several paper plates.

"You've done this before?" I ask, amazed at his efficiency.

"We do movie nights all the time. Though I'm still trying to get her to let me watch some rated-R movies."

"Sounds about right." I run a hand along my jaw. "Think we can get all this set up in an hour?"

"Easily. Do you have a laptop? Or an HDMI cord?"

"Laptop, yes. Not sure about that other thing," I say, walking over to my work bag to pull out my computer.

"It's cool, I brought an extra just in case," he says, digging through his backpack. He scans the room. "Can I hook into those speakers?" he asks, pointing at my surround sound setup. I remember having to bribe Mike to come over and set it up for me right after I moved in.

"Yep. I'm not sure what all the cords go to though, so I don't think I'll be able to reconnect everything when we're done."

"I can swing by and reset it for you, or I can text you a video with instructions."

"That would be great. Your mom has my number so whatever works, as long as you dumb it down for me. No naming HQBI cords, just say the red cord plugs into this spot."

I watch as he sits on the couch, boots everything up, and has an image projected on my empty wall in minutes. "You're really good at all that computer stuff, huh?"

He shrugs as he continues tapping the keys. "I got into it because of my dad."

"Is he in the tech field?"

"No? Kinda. He runs his own company. When he and my mom were together, he was always at work, and I'd hear him complain about the guys running his app and how they 'didn't know what they're doing.' I figured if I could learn about it and fix it for him, he'd be home more."

This poor kid just wanted his father's attention, and it reminds me of my own failures with Avery. I've got to do better. I don't want her starting fires in hopes that I'll show up and be around more. I doubt she'd go that far, but given our past and her grief, anything is possible when I'm all she has left.

Isaac huffs, his breath blowing the strands of his floppy, dirty-blond hair out of his face. "Don't tell my mom, but my dad's kind of a dick. All he cares about is work, and he's never around on his weekends. I mean, he buys me stuff and that's cool, but it's so boring at his place. And he's dating this new chick, so when he is around, he's spending time with her."

"He leaves you alone at his house?"

"No, there's usually staff there, or he just shoves an iPad at me, and they go hang out in another wing of the house. I might as well be home alone."

And here I am taking up all his mom's time and attention. "I'm sorry, man," I start, but trail off, not sure what I'm apologizing for. His shitty situation with his dad, or the fact that I'm stealing his mom's focus from him.

"It's not your fault." He shrugs again as he plugs in the last cord, and the opening song to *The Grinch* filters through the speakers.

"Did your mom tell you to pick that one?" I try to hide the smile on my face.

"Yeah, she said it was important that you 'watch the movie of your people?' I dunno. She's weird."

"That sounds like her," I say.

"Are you guys dating?" he asks, abruptly changing the subject.

I open and shut my mouth several times, unsure how to answer his question. Bella and I haven't discussed what we are. I would love to date her, but I don't know if the school would allow it. But we've already violated any rules that may exist after the other night. And I haven't talked to Avery about it yet either.

"It's okay if you are. You don't have to hide it," he says.

"It's not that we're hiding anything, we just haven't discussed it yet."

"But it's more than just a school project?"

"It is. I think? I want it to be, but it's complicated."

"I think you make her happier. And I like it when she's happy," he admits.

"Because you're hoping she'll let you watch rated-R movies?"

He laughs. "Think I could get you to plead my case?"

"Already trying to pit us against each other." I shake my head in mock frustration.

"Gotta keep all my options open." He smiles as the music stops and points to the screen. "All you have to do is pull up your streaming service here, and it will project the whole screen onto the wall. Just click this to make it full screen and that's it."

"Seems easy enough."

"We could watch something now, before she gets back." His voice is teasing, but there's a hint of hope there.

"Nice try." I move the mouse around, following the steps he gave as I get another movie to play.

"See, you got it. I guess old people can learn new tricks."

"That's not how the saying goes."

"Close enough."

We sit there in awkward silence as the opening sequence to *The Polar Express* plays.

"You would be okay if I did date your mom?" I ask cautiously, his earlier words floating in my head about his dad's new girlfriend stealing his focus away. The last thing I want to do is make this kid feel like he's got no one in his corner.

"Yeah. I think she likes you. I hear her talk about you a lot to her friends."

That warms my heart more than it should.

"I want you to know that you come first to your mom. No matter what, you are her priority."

"I know I am, but I don't need her hovering all the time. So, if you want to take her out on dates, I'm cool with that."

"I know we've been hanging out a lot the last month with

all this Santa stuff, but I don't want you to feel like she doesn't have time for you, though. I know you just said you feel that way at your dad's. I won't tell her about that, but I also don't want to put you in that same position."

"Totally not the same."

I wait for him to say more, but when he doesn't, I lift a brow at him.

"My dad has always been like that. I've always had to fight for his attention. Not Mom. In fact, I could use a little less of hers sometimes. I have a life too, and I want to hang out with my friends. But I know she loves me."

"He may have a shitty way of showing it, but I'm sure your dad loves you too."

He shrugs again. "He loves the idea of having a kid and having someone to hand his business to one day. It's not the same."

My stomach twists at his words, and I try to school the expression on my face. Concern for him, but also worry over Avery looking at our relationship like that one day.

"I wish I had a dad like you."

My head whips in his direction.

"Look at everything you're doing for Avery. My dad would never go through all of this for me. But my mom would. And if you'd do all this for Avery, you'd do all this for my mom, and she deserves someone like that."

———

Later that night, Avery is tucked against me as we lay on the blankets and pillows on the living room floor. There's popcorn and crumbs everywhere. She spilled two sodas before I put it in an old sippy cup I found buried in the cabinets. And I spend more time watching her than I do the movie.

Once the credits roll, we gather up the blankets and take them outside to shake off the crumbs on the porch before I throw them in the washer. Avery's just finished brushing her teeth when she walks into her room and climbs into her bed where I'm waiting for her.

"Did you have fun, baby girl?"

"Yup!" she says through a yawn. I sit there, stroking her hair, deliberating how to talk to her about Bella.

"What do you think about Daddy having a girlfriend?" I ask, and when I see her brows furrow, I tack on, "One day."

"Does that mean I have to share you with someone else like the fire people?"

Something cracks in my chest at her words, and I know what I have to do, even if the thought of it hurts more than anything has in quite a while.

CHAPTER 13
BELLA

On Monday morning before class starts, Avery comes running up to me full of excitement.

"Miss Carlisle, guess what we did yesterday!"

"I don't know, what did you do?" I totally played that off, I think to myself.

"My daddy made a movie theater in my house, and we had candy and popcorn, and he let me have the fizzy soda."

"That's amazing, Avery. What movie did you watch?"

"We watched *The Santa Clause*."

"That's a good one." My heart somersaults in my chest at her words. Not only did he listen to my lesson, but he immediately took action for her. Fuck, do I love a man with follow-through. I mean, like. I *like* him. I really fucking like him. But not love. It's way too soon for that. Right?

There's commotion from across the room, and we turn in that direction.

"They're back! Look, they're back!" Cade squeals.

It's the first of December, which means my shelf is now the home of two little elves, one boy and one girl.

And after a lively debate, the class settled on Jingles McTwinkles and Bubbly Sparklepants. Don't ask me whose name belongs to who. Several students start arguing over who gets to take the elves home, and I clap my hands to get their attention. "I was thinking that since we only have three weeks before winter break and there are more of you than there are weeknights, we could divide and conquer."

"We can't split them up!" Micah shouts, and I let out a resigned sigh, knowing this is going to derail my lesson plan for the day.

"Can we come up with our own elf names?" Penny asks.

"We already named our elves," I say.

She shakes her head. "No, I mean for us. Like we have our name and our elf name."

"I want an elf name!" Micah shouts.

"Me too!" Cade adds.

Pretty soon, the whole class is whining for an elf name, and I decide, fuck it, this is how we're spending the rest of our day. I quickly print out some holiday coloring sheets and disperse them as kids come up one by one, and I look up possible elf names that are unique to each of their personalities.

When it's Avery's turn, she walks over with a nervous look on her face.

"Ready to pick out your elf name?" I ask.

She nods, and I turn back to my computer. "First, I'm going to look up the meaning of your name so we can find one that suits you best." I stifle a laugh when I find out the meaning of Avery. *Ruler of the elves*. This is perfect. And then it hits me. No wonder she was so upset when her elf didn't show up last year.

"Do you know what your name means?"

"I'm the ruler of the elves." Something pinches in my chest at the pained look on her face. "Mommy used to call me 'Elf Princess.' It was her secret nickname for me. Daddy doesn't know." Her hands clench at her sides like she's trying to squeeze back the tears with her fists.

"What's wrong, sweetie?"

"I need a hug, but you always say that's not allowed. But you hugged me at my house, and my body feels like it needs a hug." Her voice is small as she fidgets with her hands.

"We're not supposed to, but I think one hug will be okay," I say, pulling her against me. I try to make it a quick one, but she refuses to let go.

"I miss my mommy."

Something cracks in my chest at her words. This is the first time I've seen the broken little girl grieving her mom, and I'm reminded more than ever how important my Santa lessons are.

———————

School is almost out for the day, and I head down the hallway to pick up my class from their elective when I spot a tall, dark, and handsome firefighter.

"Hey, you're early. I thought we were meeting after school?" I say as I try my best not to check him out. You're at work. His daughter's school. *Behave.*

"I'm working some earlier shifts this week, so I thought I'd come up here and knock out some of the construction. Think Isaac would want to help?" he asks. There's something off about his tone and demeanor, but I chalk it up to us being at the school. It's not like we could just start groping each other here. That would be inappropriate, even if it's taking every-thing in me not to do just that.

"Power tools aren't really his thing. But he could design you anything on a computer."

"I'll keep that in mind for future projects," he says with a mischievous smile. I wonder what that's about?

"I wanted to tell you about something that happened in class today. We were coming up with elf names, and Avery got upset about a nickname her mom used to call her and mentioned missing her mom."

He drags a hand through his stubble. "Shit, is she okay?"

"I think so, but I wanted to let you know."

"What was the nickname?"

"I found out her name means 'ruler of the elves' and she told me her mom used to call her Elf Princess. It might explain why she got so upset about her elf not showing up."

He mouths "Fuck" as he tugs on his neck and drops his eyes, a war of emotions on his face. "I messed up more than I realized."

"It's okay, we can fix this. You have me."

His eyes flick up to mine, and he raises his eyebrows. "I'm really glad I went to that PTO meeting," he says.

"Well, I'm glad Lefty decided to introduce herself to you, but I could've done without the bladder infection."

He chuckles, his gaze roaming down to my chest.

"I also learned that your name means 'bold' or 'brave,' by the way, and I thought it was very fitting for you, considering what you do," I say.

"You looked up my name?" he asks, as the corner of his mouth lifts.

"I looked up a lot of names," I say, suddenly full of nervous energy. Why do I want to impress him so much?

The office door opens behind him and a student walks out, breaking the moment.

Hardy hooks a thumb over his shoulder. "I'm going to get started before school lets out. Are we still meeting in your room after?"

"Actually, I thought I might take Avery shopping to cheer her up and pick up something for your next Santa lesson. Can Isaac hang out with you for a little bit?"

"He can. Let me give you some money so you can get what you need." He reaches for his wallet and hands me a wad of cash.

Fanning out the bills, I decide to have a little fun with him. I can tell something is up. It feels like he's pulling back from our connection, and I'm determined to loosen him up. "Hmm, the pet food might cost a little more."

He quirks a brow. "I don't like the sound of that. I want it on record that I'm opting out of pets on our Santa tier."

I shake my head in laughter. "Noted." And then I walk off as he shouts behind me.

"Bella? Seriously, no pets. Not even a goldfish!"

I wave a hand in the air as I head down the hall. Once the bell rings, and the last student leaves my room, I get Avery's booster seat out of Hardy's truck and load her up in my car.

We're off to get gingerbread supplies at the Chestnut Mountain Market. We walk through the aisles as Avery excitedly weighs her options between glitter sprinkles and Christmas tree-shaped ones.

"I think we should go with the glitter since it will make the house pop."

"Can we make trees for the house too?" Avery asks, with the biggest, roundest eyes I've ever seen. How does Hardy say no to this?

"What would we use?"

She rubs at her jaw the same way I've seen Hardy do a few times, and it sets off butterflies in my stomach at the thought of him.

"We could use an ice cream cone. The pointy kind and glue the tree sprinkles to it."

"I think that's an excellent idea!"

We spend way too much time in the candy and baking aisles, and it's nearly dark when we leave the store.

> Headed back to your house now. You and Isaac on your way?

> He's helping me clean up now, then we're out the door

> You've got a good one

My mama heart warms at the praise. Isaac and I may have an unconventional relationship, full of oversharing and shenanigans, but I love that kid and I wouldn't trade him for the world.

We pull into Hardy's driveway within minutes of each other, and the boys help us carry all our bags inside.

"Jeez, Mom. Did you buy the whole store?"

Hardy offers me a grateful smile. I'm determined to make this a memorable experience for him and Avery, and I hope he can see that in my face and in the multiple shopping bags on his kitchen table.

It's a team effort as we dump all the contents onto the table and begin organizing ingredients.

"Gingerbread houses?" Hardy asks.

"Yeah, you got a problem with them?"

"No, I'm just surprised you use the kits. You strike me as the kind of person that would bake all that from scratch."

"Gingerbread is trash. These are for decoration, not eating. There is no point in spending all that time baking to not eat it after. It's also why we're making them so early. The Christmas cookie session will come closer to Christmas," I whisper the last part, so Avery doesn't hear.

"I like gingerbread," Avery says.

"Then you can eat yours if your dad says it's okay. But go wash your hands before we get started. You too, Isaac."

Isaac grumbles as he follows Avery into the bathroom.

"She's gonna fill up on all the candy we use to decorate and won't have room for the house or the trees. That's why I always stock up on extra beyond what the kits come with, because eating the decorations is half the fun."

"I'm learning so much," he says with a small smirk.

An hour later, we're all a sticky, sugar-glitter covered mess, but Avery has done nothing but laugh and smile the whole time. Even my sullen teenager has gone out of his way to make sure Avery has everything she needs.

"I saw you give Avery that Kit Kat," I say out of the corner of my mouth when she's distracted.

He shrugs. "She needed more for her roof."

"It was the last one, and it's your favorite candy. It was nice, thank you."

"Shhh, you'll ruin my street cred."

"I think that went out the window when you were counting pubes."

He turns away, ignoring my jab, but I see the corner of his mouth quirk briefly into a smile.

Hardy proudly holds up his house, and as soon as he does, it collapses in on itself and he drops it onto the counter with a thud. "Son of a b—"

"Daddy!"

"Sorry, Avery."

"Need some help over there?" I tease.

"I can build a whole freaking workshop from scratch with my bare hands, but I can't figure out the right icing ratio to glue cookies together," he huffs.

It's obvious he's getting worked up, so I walk over to him and place a hand on his upper back, rubbing small circles as I lower my voice so only he can hear. "You're doing an amazing job, Hardy. Don't be so hard on yourself. Avery hasn't stopped smiling this whole time."

"Really? Now I feel like an ass because I was too focused on my house to notice. There are too many distractions. My focus should be on her," he huffs, and a knot of emotion forms in my throat, trying not to read deeper into his words.

"She doesn't expect perfection from you, just your presence. The important thing is you're doing it together. That's what matters."

"I'm not good at this," he admits.

"No parent is. We just figure it out along the way and hope we don't fuck up our kid too bad in the process."

He chuckles and then leans against the sink, dropping his

head as he blows out a breath. Once he collects himself, we start cleaning up the mess as the kids wash up and plop onto the couch to watch TV. I watch as Avery slowly climbs along the couch until she's snuggled into Isaac's side. I elbow Hardy and tilt my head toward them. I swear there's a twinkle in his eye when he watches them, but he shakes it off and continues cleaning up the kitchen.

Something's changed in the last few days, and I can feel him pulling away. I try not to let it bother me, but it's the last thought in my brain as I drift off to sleep that night.

CHAPTER 14
HARDY

omehow, I keep finding myself alone with this woman, and I'm having a damn hard time trying to stop myself from taking exactly what I know we both want. But I shouldn't complicate things. She teaches my daughter. If we start something and it doesn't work out, I don't want to put Avery in the middle of it. Avery has to come first. And her words from the other night keep playing on a loop in my head.

"Does that mean I have to share you with someone else like the fire people?"

And what if Bella sees how broken I really am and decides I'm not worth the trouble? I have a lot of baggage, and I don't want to subject her to it. And what if she thinks less of me when she finds out what I've done? But I don't think she'd push me away. There's just something about her that feels safe. Like home.

But this back-and-forth is wearing on me, and I know she's picking up on it. I'm not sure how much longer I can resist her.

Two days after the gingerbread-house-that-couldn't, we're at Bella's for another planning session while Avery is with the sitter since we don't want her to see this part of Santa's Workshop. Isaac is at a friend's house which means we're alone.

We've spent most of the afternoon sorting items that we collected at the firehouse drop-off box into piles, deciding what's usable and what category it should be in.

I can't stop staring at this woman's ass in her shorts every time she bends over to place a toy in a pile, and I know she's caught on to my leering. It's almost become a game where she'll pick up a toy, saunter across the room, and then slowly bend to place it in the pile. It's not the most efficient way to sort shit, but I'm not complaining.

Grabbing a handful out of the box, I carefully drop each item into the appropriate pile. When I look over at Bella, she's now bending over with her butt away from me, but I can see all the way down her shirt.

Fuck me. Why can't I be with her, again?

"Something you want to talk about, Grumpy Gus?" She stands and crosses her arms under her breasts, pushing them up as they spill slightly out of the top of her shirt.

"Nope," I say, as I try to ignore the vixen tempting the last of my willpower.

"Doesn't sound like nothing. You keep looking over here and grumbling."

I toss the last stuffed animal in my hand into the pile and sink onto the couch as I prop my arms on my knees and bury my face in my hands, blowing out the last of my resolve in a long, slow breath.

When I open my eyes, she's standing in front of me, and I look up into her blue eyes. Eyes that are so light blue, they're almost grey. Eyes that are looking down at me with hunger.

She puts a hand on my shoulder to shove me back against the couch and then slowly sits down, straddling my lap.

"I've seen you staring at me all afternoon. Little glances here and there. Why do you think I'm taking my sweet time going through that box?"

My heart races in my chest and I worry she can hear it as I

shrug, unwilling to answer her question. Be strong. Resist the hot teacher.

"Not a day has gone by that I don't think about the way you manhandled me in that storage closet. The way your tongue did acrobatics against mine. Or the way you ate me on the couch. I'm tired of bending over waiting for you to make a move. I'm almost thirty-five. I can't keep bending like that without paying for it tomorrow."

I chuckle as I rub my hands along her outer thighs. "So that would make you a nineties baby, huh? I was born in the previous decade, and you don't see me complaining."

"Yeah, but you literally work out for a living so you can do all the manly fire shit. And you don't look a decade older than me."

My stomach knots at her words. If only she knew how bad I actually was at that fire shit when it mattered most. I swallow down the nerves, trying to keep things lighthearted. "I didn't say I was that much older than you, just born in the decade before you."

"What year?"

"Eighty-nine."

"Ah, the year of our lord and savior, Taylor Swift. And seriously, you're like a year older than me." She laughs as her hands stroke up my chest. The air grows thick between us as I stare at her. My eyes focus on her plush lips as she leans in and kisses me.

I let it go on far longer than I should as she winds her hands around my neck and makes little circles against me with her hips. I'm only a man—a weak, weak man who is tired of pushing away the one thing I want most.

She breaks the kiss and trails her lips along my jaw, around my neck, until she finally lands on a spot near my collarbone that has me bucking up against her.

"Fuck. We need to stop," I say reluctantly as I grab her arms and hold her away from me.

"What's wrong? Did you not like that?" I can see the insecurities building in her head. I pull her off my lap and stand as I start pacing the living room.

"I can't do this. We can't do this," I say, stopping to wave a hand between us.

"There are no school rules preventing it, if that's what you're worried about. I checked. And I can clearly see your enthusiasm outlined in your pants, so that's not the issue either."

"It's not that." I turn my back to her as I try to calm the storm of emotions swirling inside of me, like my grief is the offensive line and here comes my lust, trampling all over it like a defensive line blocking a winning play. What the fuck is wrong with me? She wants this. I want this. I want *her*. But I can't—I can't get more attached. I can see myself falling for this woman, and the thought of losing her already terrifies me. What if I can't save her? What if something happens to her, and I can't get there fast enough?

"Then, what is it?" There's a teasing quality to her voice, but I can hear her frustration too. "Please enlighten me, because I'm tired of your grump calling the shots here. I don't know how I can be any more obvious, but I'm going to lay it all out, because what the hell else do I have to lose at this point? My dignity went out the window the minute we met, so clearly…"

She trails off, and I turn to face her, curious to know how she was going to finish that thought. "Clearly what?"

"I like you. I might more than fucking like you. And I can't believe I just admitted that."

"I more than fucking like you too," I say, taking a step toward her.

"Then, what is the problem?" she asks, exasperated.

"I can't fall for you."

She winces, and the hurt on her face makes a knot form in my chest.

"I'm the reason why Avery doesn't have a mom. It's *my* fault. And now I'm raising her on my own, and I'm fucking that up too. I'm trying to split my time between her and work, but there's not enough of me to go around and Avery's noticed. I don't think she's okay with me sharing any more of my time beyond her and work."

"That's a lot of information to unpack. Can we start with the part where you think it's your fault that her mom died?" She looks at me expectantly, but there's something in her eyes that makes me want to tell her everything, and at this moment I know that she can handle what I'm about to throw at her.

I sit next to her on the couch and drop my head into my hands. "There was a fire at a boutique clothing store in Denver. It was a busy day, and I'd gone out on another call when it came in. It turns out Lydie snuck out on her lunch break to pick up some things. I didn't know she was there." I take a deep breath, willing myself to continue as a rush of shame washes over me. "She was supposed to be at work, but apparently, she was in the store when it caught fire, and the building collapsed before they could get her out."

"Oh my God, Hardy." She moves closer to me, placing a comforting hand on my thigh.

My voice wobbles as I continue. "She died in a *fire*, and I wasn't there." I inhale sharply as I fight back the tears I rarely shed. I press my pointer fingers into the corners of my eyes. "I should have been there. I could have gotten to her. It's all my fucking fault my little girl doesn't have a mom. I'm a fire-fighter, and I couldn't save my wife from a fire."

"Oh, Hardy. I can't even begin to imagine that pain and guilt you've endured. But this wasn't your fault. You know that, right?" She pulls me into a hug, rubbing a hand along my spine in long strokes as I let go of the guilt and fear I've been holding in for nearly two years. Deep shuddering breaths wrack my body as I fight back the tears, but it's no use. They spill out of me, dampening her shirt as I press my face into her shoulder. "I need you to know this wasn't your fault. Even if you had been there, there's no guarantee you could have gotten her out, and then Avery could have lost both of her parents that day."

"I'm sorry, it's hard for me to talk about this."

"Have you ever talked to a therapist about it?" she asks, pulling back to look at my face.

I nod. "There was this widower's support group I went to in Denver before we moved out here, and it helped. Avery has a therapist, and we do family sessions sometimes, and I do have a therapist."

"Then you should know that none of that was your fault. You did the best you could with the information you had at the time. That's all you could do. As awful as that experience was, I bet it made you a better firefighter. You're probably hypervigilant. I bet it's the reason why you were promoted to lieutenant so quickly."

Fuck, I think she has a point.

"You can say it."

I raise an eyebrow in confusion.

"It's written all over your face. Just give me those two little words that make every woman instantly wet."

"…good girl?"

She laughs, and it goes straight to my dick. "No, tell me I'm right."

A much-needed laugh escapes me as I smile at her. "You're right."

"That's it, talk dirty to me, Hardy. Tell me how right I am."

I throw my head back in laughter. "How do you do that? I've never met anyone like you. You have this ability to see the bright side in every situation. And make anything sound dirty."

"It's called optimism, and the rest is because I'm a pervert." She laughs as her eyes connect with mine. "I know it might be surprising for a grump like you, but not all of us see the glass as half empty. It might shock you to learn that I wasn't always this way."

Placing a hand on her thigh, I focus all my attention on her.

"When I was eighteen, I lost my mom in a terrible car accident. She was driving, and I was in the passenger seat. At first, I felt so much guilt because we were fighting right before the crash and I blamed myself, but the roads were icy, and we would've crashed regardless. It took a while for me to see how her death made me stronger. And it doesn't mean that I'm glad that my mom died, or that you lost your wife and Avery lost her mom. But those experiences make us stronger people. They teach us lessons we need to know, as painful as they may be. And they shape us into the people we're meant to become. Trust me, there's a part of me that would give anything to have her back, to have had that crash never happen, but I also wouldn't be the woman I am today, and I know my mom would be so proud of who I've grown into. And I know that if she had the choice, she'd pick this version of me, even if she had to sacrifice herself to make it happen. That's what we do as moms. We love our kids more than ourselves, and I didn't know Lydie, but something tells me she would have done the same."

She totally would have.

I think through her words. "I don't deserve you."

"No one does, but I'll take you anyway," she says with a smile.

"Who knew there was so much heart under that perfect boob."

"Aww, you think my boobs are perfect?" She flutters her eyelashes as I lean back on the couch, crossing my arms.

"Just the left one. I've only seen the right one once, so I might need more exposure to really form an opinion." I wink at her. What the fuck am I doing, and since when do I *wink*? Then again, this woman has me doing all sorts of things out of my comfort zone.

"We can totally make that happen," she says, arching her perfect eyebrow. I feel myself leaning in toward her, as though we're magnets that can no longer stay apart.

But then her phone rings. She throws her head back and groans. "Why must you dangle the literal carrot in front of me?"

She leans over to the coffee table and answers it. "Isaac?"

My brow furrows and my alarm bells go up at her tone.

"No, no, it's okay. I'll be right there." Once she hangs up, she looks at me apologetically. "So, I don't want you to think this is a sign or anything, because I totally wanted to see where this was headed, but Isaac said he wants to come home and I need to go pick him up."

"But he's okay? Everything's okay?" I ask, trying to calm my nerves.

She holds my face in her hands and kisses the top of my nose. "Everything is fine. Just a moody teen. And we will pick up where we left off tomorrow. It's already Wednesday, and we've only checked gingerbread off my emoji list." She sighs. "Nothing ruins hump day like not getting humped."

I smile as I nod against her face, thankful for her ability to ease the tension. "Tomorrow."

Tell me why the thought of seeing her tomorrow suddenly feels like too long a wait. I'd nearly convinced myself to end things with her, but after our confessions, it feels like something has shifted between us. She pulls my lips to hers and kisses me tenderly, before blowing raspberries against my closed mouth and throwing her head back in laughter. I could get addicted to this. To her heart and her chaos. And while I cherish the memories I have of Lydie, I'm excited at the idea of creating something new with Bella. Now I need to get my head out of my ass and step up my game.

CHAPTER 15
HARDY

"If it isn't my favorite firefighter," Bella says, leaning against my open window in the carpool line the next afternoon as Avery hops in the back seat.

"What are you doing later?" I ask.

"I was going to finish sorting inventory. Why?" Her mouth crooks up on one side as she studies my face for clues.

"About that list you texted me… I know it's your thing and all, but I found this spot while out on a call today. Even though it's a school night, it's the perfect weather for this, and I wanted to take some of the burden off you. You've been doing so much, I figured it'd be nice to plan something for you for a change. Plus, I don't know if you'll find a cooler spot to skate," I say as her face lights up.

"We're going skating?" Between the way I pout my lip and the excitement in Avery's voice, there's no way she's going to deny us.

"I would love to." Bella seems genuinely surprised, and it fills me with pride to know that I did that.

"Yes!" comes a cheer from the back seat.

"Great! We'll pick you and Isaac up in an hour. Dress warm. Oh, and eat first. There aren't a lot of food options where we're going, and I don't know how late we'll get back," I call out as she heads back into the school.

I can't get Avery to finish her plate on a good night, but right now that's damn near impossible as she flits around, talking excitedly. It's all I can do to get her to take a bite before she's up and spinning around the room again.

When we get to Bella's, I'm barely in the driveway when she's out the door with Isaac close behind. He's holding a giant thermos in his hands as he climbs into the truck behind me.

"Hey, Butterfly," Isaac says to Avery.

"Hi, Giraffe."

"Giraffe?" he questions.

"Yeah, because you're tall and sometimes you have spots on your face."

I struggle to hold it in, refusing to make eye contact with Bella or I'm going to lose the fight with my laughter. Instead, I look at Isaac in the rearview mirror, and he shrugs.

"So where are we headed?" Bella asks.

"Vixen Lake. You know it? It's near Dasher Lane, off Prancer Road." My smile is teasing as I check the rearview.

"Look at you being a comedian. Hardy har har. Oh my gosh, get it? Hardy har har?"

I hand her the phone with the address put in and slowly back out of the driveway. "Just point me in the right direction."

"Haven't you figured out that I've been doing that this whole time?" Her face turns to mine, and I return her smile as I pull onto the road.

"Are you sure there's a lake out here?" Avery asks as we climb the steep gravel road. It's a struggle to keep from sliding around, and I'm suddenly glad we took my truck.

"There is. It's a little bit of a haul, but I promise it's worth it."

We hit a particularly slick patch of ice and fishtail a little as I struggle to keep control of the vehicle.

"Mom, are you okay?" Isaac asks from the back seat.

"What's wrong?" I ask, trying to keep the panic out of my voice as I keep my eyes on the road.

"Isaac, sit back and keep your seatbelt on," she barks, and the hairs on the back of my neck prickle with her tone. Something's wrong. And then I remember. Her mom, the accident. I put my hazards on and pull to the side of the road.

"Why are we stopping?" Avery whines.

"What are you doing?" Bella asks, sounding out of breath.

"I'll be right back," I say as I hop out of the cab and walk around the truck, pulling a bag of salt out of the covered truck bed. I sprinkle it in front of me as I walk until I'm fifty feet away from the vehicle throwing salt over the rough patch we just hit. I hustle back to the truck and throw the last of the salt down in front of the vehicle for good measure and climb back in, shoving the empty salt bag under the seat.

"Didn't want to hit the same patch on the way down," I explain.

She gives me a watery smile, and I merge back onto the road. We pull into a wooded area a few minutes later. It takes entirely too long to get Avery bundled up. Isaac's no better, insisting that he's fine in a hoodie.

We walk down to the edge of the pond, and I remove several pairs of skates from a duffle bag I stowed in the truck bed. She looks at me in confusion as I pass them out. "How did you—"

"Know your sizes?" I smile as she bends to help Avery strap her tiny skates on. "I texted Isaac, and he told me your size and where I could find skates to rent locally. That kid's a whiz on the computer."

She finishes tying the skate and then walks over to me, pulling my ear close to her mouth. "You have no idea how bad I want to bang you right now."

"Because of ice skates?" I ask.

"Because you made magic happen. For me and my kid." She

leans against me to pull on her skates, and I watch as Avery toddles toward Isaac and he helps her onto the ice. Meanwhile, I try to slow my beating heart. "I was starting to think you were having second thoughts about us. I probably could've just asked you point-blank, but sometimes that's not how my brain works."

Her honesty pierces through my armor and I loop an arm around her waist, pulling her against me. "I'm so consumed with thoughts of you it's become a problem," I admit. Then I release Bella, remembering Avery's words. "There was something I didn't tell you last night."

"About Lydie?"

I shake my head. "About something Avery said the other night when I was tucking her in. I asked her if she would be okay with me having a girlfriend, and she asked if that meant she'd have to share me with someone like she shares me with the firehouse."

"And? Was she okay with it?"

"I… I don't know. I kind of shut down when she said that and didn't ask any follow-up questions."

"If I've learned anything about that little girl over the past few months, it's that she asks a *lot* of questions. But it's because she's curious about how the world works. I don't think she was saying that she wasn't okay with it. I think that was her way of processing what could be a big change in her life. You should talk to her about it."

Lacing up my skates, I mull over her words, but I don't have much time to think before Bella's tugging me onto the ice with her. "I've never done this before," I admit as she grips my hands and skates backwards in front of me.

"I can tell," she says with a laugh, and at this point it's more her pulling me while I glide along, trying my best not to twist an ankle.

"There are death blades strapped to my feet and I'm freezing my ass off. Not to mention the fact that I'm terrified any one of us will fall through the ice. But I'm doing it anyway…for you."

Her face lights up in the widest smile. "Aww, you're grumpy even when you're being nice. Don't worry, the lake is shallow, so it doesn't take much to freeze it solid. And I've lived here most of my life and have never heard of anyone going through the ice."

"Is this where you planned to take us skating?" I ask. I nearly slip, but she stiffens her arms to steady me. It feels good to lean on her for support, as natural as a spark taking to kindling.

"Careful there, big fella. Actually, I'd forgotten about this place until you mentioned it today. I haven't been here since I was a kid. My plans would've had us driving out to Denver to go to a local rink."

I look up as the first snowflake hits my nose and pinch my brows at the darkening sky. Suddenly, the lake is illuminated by strings of Christmas lights hung on posts around the perimeter.

When I look over at Avery, she's grinning ear to ear, pointing at the lights as Isaac skates behind her, hands on her shoulders, steadying her each time it looks like she's going to fall.

"This is magical, like something out of a movie," Bella says, awestruck as she takes everything in.

I clear my throat. "You deserve someone to make magic for you considering how much you do for everyone else."

Her gaze connects with mine and her eyebrow arches in challenge, so I speak before she can turn it into a dick joke. "I know you think your life's a disaster and you joke about being a hot mess, but that's not what I see."

"What do you see?"

"I see an incredibly selfless woman who would do anything for the people she cares about."

She shrugs, her grip tightening on mine. "You needed help. I like to help."

"But who helps you?" I ask. Her eyes drop to the ice, and I worry I've struck a nerve. She's still skating backwards, pulling my clumsy ass along, so I continue. "It feels like I should be doing more. You do so much."

"You act like you're doing nothing. You're building an entire North Pole in the gym."

"It's not enough, not considering the entire list of activities you've planned for us. I want to help take some of the load off you."

"I'd like you to put your load inside me."

My chest vibrates with laughter. It's a struggle to compose myself, and I look over at the kids for a distraction. I can't stop smiling at Avery as she squeals and bosses Isaac around.

Bella squeezes my hand. "That's why I do it, for moments like that. Look at her face. It's not a burden when you're having fun. She's worth it, and you both deserve to be happy."

Fighting back the guilt, I nod my head. "She is worth it," I say, my eyes finally meeting hers. "But so are you. You give so much to those around you and yet you're so hard on yourself. You didn't have to help me, but you did anyway, and I appreciate that, but I want to step up my game. I may not have all The Santa Rules figured out yet, but I can do more."

Her responding smile warms my heart.

We spend another thirty minutes out on the ice before Avery's teeth start chattering. We take off our skates as Isaac runs to the truck to get the thermos. Each of us have a cup of hot chocolate, and as I drink mine, my mind wanders back to my movie night with Bella.

"Your ears are red, and I can't figure out if it's the cold or if you're having dirty thoughts," Bella whispers to me. I pull her against me, running my hand up and down her arm to warm her up.

"I'm just thinking about other places I'd like to lick hot chocolate off you," I say, as my eyes drift down to her cocoa.

"You better not be thinking about putting that anywhere else."

My brow quirks in confusion.

"I would prefer to not get a UTI, thank you, and if you put that anywhere near my lady parts, that's for sure what'll happen. That stuff is just for nipples or book boyfriends, nothing else." Her laugh is infectious as I pull her closer.

"Um, Hardy?" she rasps against my ear.

"Yeah?"

"Is that your phone in your pocket, or are you just happy to see me?"

"Not my phone," I say, pulling the carrot from my pocket.

"Oh my God, was that in there the whole time?" Her voice is teasing as she eyes the vegetable.

"I shoved it in my pocket when I pulled the skates from the truck bed."

"Can we build a snowman?" Avery asks, running over and snatching the carrot out of my hand.

In unison, everyone looks at me for approval. "I guess we're making a snowman."

An unspoken understanding passes between the three of us as we take turns helping Avery make each giant snowball. Time passes surprisingly quickly, and before I know it, we've got a finished snowman with rocks for a mouth and eyes, sticks for arms, and a carrot for the nose. We snap dozens of pictures at Avery's request and pile back into the car, carefully making our way down the mountain so we can get home in time for my little girl's bedtime.

When we pull into the driveway, it hits me that I don't want Bella or Isaac to leave. They've folded so naturally into our lives. Now, I just need to talk to Avery, when she's not so sleepy, and figure out how to ease her mind about us dating. If

Bella can manage work, raising a kid, and seeing me, surely, I can figure out how to do it too.

CHAPTER 16
BELLA

I'm locked in and laser-focused on my lesson plans when an unexpected visitor interrupts me the next day.

"We need to talk," Amber's nasal voice calls out from the door of my classroom. I make a sweeping gesture with my hand to invite her in.

"Is this about the workshop? We have inventory almost sorted and we were under budget."

She saunters into the room, holding something in her hand. "Do you know what this is?"

"Sorry, I have a lot of work to do and a short planning period, so can you just tell me so I can help with whatever it is?" I try to sound sweet, but this woman is grating on my nerves.

"Something in the paper caught my eye last weekend." She unfolds the clipping in her hands, holding up the ad that Raven ran for me.

"You do forget that Chuck works down at the Chestnut Mountain Newspaper, and he showed me your little ad. It's so trashy that you think selling used goods is acceptable." She tsks me, like I'm a dog who disappointed her by peeing on her rug.

"Not everything is used, and everything we've received so far is in good shape. I assure you it's not going to be a tacky garage sale with random used goods and neon stickers." Why am I defending myself to this woman?

Amber places a hand on her hip. "I knew you'd mess this up. You ruin everything you touch, just like your marriage."

I swallow down the anger rising in my throat and tack on a fake smile as I stand from my desk and walk over to her. "I know you aren't coming into my classroom to tell me how to do things. You needed help with the workshop; I'm helping with it. You don't get a say in how Hardy and I run things. And as far as my marriage goes, it takes two people to mess that up and it was long over before your husband started running his mouth. And I might have been the best he's ever had, but his performance was honestly forgettable. So, unless you're here for pointers about how to please him in the bedroom, I suggest you leave so I can get back to lesson planning."

She huffs several times, looking stunned that I would speak to her like that. Honestly, I'm stunned too as I hide my shaking hands behind my back. Normally, I'd take her vitriol and let it roll off me, but she made it personal, and I couldn't bite my tongue anymore.

"This isn't over," she spits.

"*This isn't over*," I mimic. "Seriously, Amber, do you hear yourself? This is for the kids. This isn't some movie where you're the hero trying to expose some evil plot I'm master-minding. You're being a dick."

Her mouth drops open, and she turns and stomps off, her heels clicking extra loud as she goes.

"Umm, what was that about?" Lucy says, popping her head into my room.

"How long were you standing there?"

"Long enough to hear you call Amber a dick." She walks over to my desk and sits in one of the chairs.

"Are your kids at recess right now?"

"Yup, inside recess in the gym. Too cold for outdoor recess. So, I've got about ten minutes for you to fill me in, then I need to make copies before they come back."

"She saw the ad Raven ran about the donations. I totally forgot Chuck works at the paper."

Lucy winces. "Shoot, we shoulda planned that better. Is that why she's mad?"

"Yup. Oh, and she said I'm to blame for my divorce, and that's how she knows I'm going to mess this up too."

She shoots up from her chair, looking toward the door. "She did not."

I tug her back into her chair. "Don't worry, I gave it right back to her. But that's why we have to make this the best workshop ever."

"Need me to rally the girls?"

"I could use your help to get everything set up once Hardy's done building the scenery. He said he could get some of the guys at the station to help too."

"So, hot firefighters will be there? Say less."

"It'll be tedious, but we need to lay all the donations out and sort them by price. There might be some painting too, I dunno. I'll have to check to see how far Hardy gets this weekend."

"Will they be shirtless? In their gear?" She stares off as if trying to picture Hardy's crew half naked.

"Focus, Lucy. There's a lot left to do."

"So how are things going with your firefighter?"

"He's not mine, not really."

"But you want him to be?"

"Yes, I want him to be, but he's working through a lot. One minute he's hot for me, and the next minute it's like he's reminded of all his responsibilities and he's pushing me away again."

"Oh, that one is definitely hot for you." She looks at her

watch. "Shoot, I gotta scoot before the second-graders return. Text me the details, and I'll gather the girls."

Several hours later, after a finger-painting incident, a meltdown over a Capri-Sun straw, and way too many runny noses walking around my room looking for tissues, my room is empty and I'm ready to head home. A familiar face appears in the window of my door, and I motion for Hardy to come in.

"Hey, I'm gonna be up here building for a bit. I wasn't sure if you were planning anything off my Santa student list tonight, but I should probably knock some of this out."

"Is Avery with the sitter?"

"She is."

"Tell Maggie she has the night off. I'm going to take her Christmas shopping."

"You don't have to do that," he says, rubbing his neck.

"I know, but I want to. Besides, you're not my only Santa student. She wants to make Christmas special for you too."

His responding smile fills me with warmth. He walks over and hands me a wad of cash from his wallet. "Here, so she can get what she wants. But no pets. And please keep the glitter to a minimum."

"No pets. But no promises on the glitter."

———————

A few hours later, we've filled up on greasy diner food and milkshakes and have stopped at three local shops. Avery's shopping list isn't long, just Hardy, a few friends, and her favorite teacher. Isaac has been a huge help, guiding her toward items for me and watching her when I was told to leave the store so they could shop. When they walk out of Bookish Wonderland, Avery is grinning ear to ear while Isaac shakes his head as he hands me back my change from the cash I gave him.

"Alright, who's left on your list?" I ask as Avery taps a finger to her chin.

"Ummm…Daddy, and my friend Penny," she says.

"I thought you got some stuff for your dad?" Isaac asks.

"For his stocking. I have to get his tree gift," she explains like it's the most obvious thing in the world.

"Well, Santa's Workshop is almost here, and you can probably get the remaining items there," I assure her.

"Oh yeah!" Avery says.

"What about you?" I look at Isaac.

"I'm good. Hardy and I are working on something for you."

"That's not ominous sounding." My heart skips a beat at the thought of the two of them, each with very different skill sets, working together to make me something. I wish Isaac's dad would spend this kind of quality time with him.

"You'll like it," Isaac assures me.

We pile in the car and head to my house to have a wrapping party. I'm not sure what time Hardy's going to be done, so we wrap all of his gifts first and set them aside as we finish wrapping the rest.

There are scraps of paper, pieces of ribbon, and glitter all over my kitchen, yet I couldn't be happier. Avery is having the best time, and even Isaac has stuck around helping her wrap while trying to avoid her every time she threatens to cover him in glitter. I think this is the longest I've seen him not be on his computer in months. He's always been good with my students, but he seems to really get along with Avery.

We're almost finished wrapping when Hardy shows up.

"Sorry it took me so long," he says as he walks in the kitchen.

"There's nothing to apologize for. We got a lot accomplished. How'd it go at the school?" I ask, getting up from the table to stand next to him.

"Good. I think everything is nearly built. It's not to code or anything, so we'll have to make sure people don't lean on it, but it'll be a good backdrop to set the mood. Now we just need to paint it."

"I might have some helpers for that." I wink. "What are you doing tomorrow? We still have a couple items to check off that list I texted you," I say, dropping my voice on the last part, curious to see if I'm going to get hot or cold Hardy.

The tips of his ears pinken. "I'll see if Maggie can hang out with Avery tomorrow afternoon."

"Can I give her the present we got her?" Avery asks excitedly.

I chuckle. "She's so excited about everything she picked out. Good luck getting her to save all her gifts till Christmas."

"Let's try to wait closer to Christmas, baby girl," Hardy says, walking over to her and leaning down to kiss her head. When he pulls back, he swipes at his lips like he has a hair stuck to them. Then he blows air through his lips, making a horse sound.

"You okay over there?"

"Glitter," he mutters.

CHAPTER 17
HARDY

I need to just do it. What am I so fucking scared of? What's the worst that could happen when the worst has already happened to you?

Blowing out a deep breath, I walk into the kitchen and see Avery sitting at the table, eating a bowl of cereal while she watches a video on her tablet. Shit, I thought I put that away last night.

"Can we talk, baby girl?"

"Okay, Daddy," she says, still glued to the screen. I wave a hand in front of it, and she looks up at me as I hit the power button to turn it off.

I have no clue how to start this. Before things go any further with Bella, I need to know that Avery is on board with it.

Taking a seat next to her, I look into her green eyes. Fuck, she has her mother's eyes. I inhale deeply, willing myself to continue. "Do you remember what we talked about the other night?"

"About washing my hands after using the potty?" she asks nervously, like she forgot to do it again.

"Not that. About Daddy having a girlfriend," I say hesitantly.

She turns back to her cereal, taking another bite as I stare at the rainbow-colored milk swirling around her bowl. "I don't want you to have a girlfriend," she says softly, still chewing.

There's a lead weight in my gut and I clasp my hands together, resting my elbows on the table. "Why not?"

She continues chewing as she thinks about her answer. "I don't want you to leave me."

I reach out and scoop her up, pulling her into my lap as I hug her against me. "Avery, baby girl, I'm never going to leave you."

"Mommy said that too," she says softly, and I can't hold back the tears. Fuck. My heart physically aches, and I squeeze her against me, as if hugging her could physically heal both of our broken hearts. She wiggles against me, moving up and wraps her arms around my neck.

"Mommy would've stayed with you forever," I whisper, trying to speak evenly around the tears. "And I'd stay with you forever if I could. But sometimes things happen that we can't control. But I promise you I will do everything in my power to stay with you as long as I can. Do you understand?"

I feel her nod against me as I rub a hand along her back, trying to soothe her sobs as her chest heaves rapidly with each breath.

"I know you miss Mommy. I miss her too, every day. No one could ever replace her. But it's also okay to let new people into our life." I wrack my brain for examples. "Like Miss Carlisle and all your new friends in class."

"And Isaac?" she asks, pulling back to look at me.

"Exactly. None of those new people replace your mom. And they bring joy and love to your life, right?"

She nods as I wipe a tear from her cheek with my thumb. "I like Isaac. And Miss Carlisle. Can she be your girlfriend?"

Inwardly my heart is doing flips, but outwardly I remain composed, afraid to get her hopes up. "Would you like that?"

"Yeah, because then I could see her all the time. And she makes you laugh."

"She's really funny, isn't she?"

"Yup. And I like that she helps with the Christmas stuff."

Shit, I didn't realize she'd picked up on how much Bella was helping.

"With our school project?"

"Yeah, but the other stuff too. The tree, and the cookie houses, and wrapping gifts. And the ice-skating. That was my favorite."

"I guess I needed help with some of that stuff, huh?"

She nods and then reaches up to hold my cheeks in her hands. "Can we make cookies?" Her excitement and the way her eyes light up are infectious, and I nod.

"I'll ask Miss Carlisle when I see her today."

"But it's Saturday."

"I'd let you come with us, but I need to go out and buy your Christmas gifts. But I promise to spend time with you today too."

"Is Maggie coming over?"

"She is."

"Can Giraffe make cookies with us too?"

"I'm sure Isaac can."

"Can I get down now?" she asks, already wiggling out of my lap. And then she's running up the stairs shouting about something she wants to show Maggie.

———

When I pull into Bella's driveway an hour later, I can't get inside fast enough, and it has nothing to do with how cold it is outside. I knock on the door, and as soon as she opens it, she pulls me inside, closes the door, and pushes my back against it.

She grabs my cheeks and pulls my lips to hers. We're stumbling back as I kick off my shoes, bumping into the closet door in the process.

"Isaac?" I ask between kisses.

She laughs against my lips. "Never thought you'd call me my son's name when your tongue is in my mouth."

"Jesus. I mean, is he here?" My hand glides up the front of her shirt, as I palm the cup of her bra.

"His dad's," she says, arching back, pushing her tit into my hand as I massage it through the fabric.

"How'd it go with Avery? Good, I take it?" she says as she peppers my neck with kisses.

"All good," I say, pulling her back into me as I cup the back of her neck and lick along the seam of her lips until she opens for me. There's a fervor in our movements that I've never experienced before, as though we can't move fast enough, can't kiss deep enough.

She jumps into my arms, and I spin her and push her up against the door right as a knock comes from the other side.

"Fuck," I groan as I drop my head on her shoulder. This is the second time something has stopped us from taking things further, and I'm starting to think it is a sign.

"It's not a sign," she says, somehow mind-reading. She extracts herself from my arms, then peeks through the peephole. "It's a delivery?"

"Is that a question?"

She opens the door to a man I don't recognize. "Ned? What are you doing here?"

"Have a delivery for ya. Where do ya want it?"

"Want what?" she asks just as two men come around the corner carrying a very large, very ornate Santa chair.

"That was supposed to go to the school," she protests, and the two men carrying the chair stop.

"It's not a problem," I say, placing a hand on her shoulder. "I can run it up there later this week."

"Want us to put it in the garage?" Ned asks.

"Yeah, lemme move my car," Bella says, grabbing her keys and shoes, leaving me with Ned.

"I hope you guys get some good use out of this. I'm happy to see it have a new home," Ned says.

"You aren't using it this year?" I ask.

"Nah, we haven't had nearly enough little visitors to make it worth hiring a Santa. Kids just don't believe like they used to. But I think putting it up at the school is the perfect spot for it. Maybe it'll help reinvigorate the magic for them," he says, clapping a hand on my shoulder as he turns to leave.

I slip on my shoes and walk outside to the garage, just as the guys are taking off after Ned.

"Ugh, I hope Amber doesn't hear about this. She already came to my classroom earlier this week to give me shit."

"The fuck?" I ask.

She waves me off. "It's fine. I handled it. Are you sure you can get this to the school by yourself?" she asks as she sinks into the massive chair.

"Not a problem. I can bring it up there this week."

"Really? I feel like you've been doing all the heavy lifting with the workshop, and I'm just telling you what to do."

"What if I like it when you boss me around?" I say, closing the garage door as she follows me with her eyes, swiveling in the seat to watch me.

I stalk back over to her slowly, my movements deliberate as the garage door slowly lowers, the only light in the space filtering in from a small window in a door in the corner.

"Is your garage light out?" I ask, looking up at the operator mounted to the ceiling.

"The light burnt out a couple years ago. I keep meaning to replace it, but I don't have a ladder."

"I'd be happy to help with that," I say, looking down at her as I hook a finger under her chin and tilt it up to me.

"You would?" she rasps as I tuck a loose hair behind her ear and then slowly sink to my knees. "What are you doing?"

"Well, you are sitting on a throne." I run my hands up her thighs as she slowly parts them. When I find the waistband of her leggings, I pull them down as she lifts her ass. "It'd be a shame to waste an opportunity to worship your pussy on a literal throne."

She kicks off her shoes and wiggles her feet a little when I get her leggings to her ankles. Once they're clear, I toss them behind me and spread her legs.

"No panties?" I quirk a brow.

"I told you, I'm an optimist."

Hooking my hands under her thighs, I pull her to the edge of the seat and bury my face in her cunt. As soon as her tangy taste hits my mouth, I groan in appreciation and eat her with enthusiasm, licking, sucking, and nipping her clit as she rocks underneath me.

"So fucking good. I've been dying for another taste. Are you going to squirt for me again?" I crook a finger inside her pussy as I stroke her G-spot.

"Oh shit!" she cries. "I am if you keep doing that."

Lowering my head, I devour her. She's so wet, making a mess on my face as I keep a steady pace, lapping and flicking her clit while I continue stroking her inner wall in a come-hither motion.

Her head falls back, a moan escaping her lips as she bucks harder against me. I want her to use me and take what she needs until she can't hold back anymore. And then I want to lick her clean. This woman makes magic wherever she goes, and I'm going to repay the favor, one orgasm at a time. An ache builds deep in my balls as I watch her fuck my face like her own personal toy, climbing higher and higher toward her climax.

"Oh God, yes. Yes, Hardy. Fuck. I'm coming!" she shouts as she squirts all over my face. Her scent is addicting, her taste perfection. I gently lick her clean, careful not to overstimulate her sensitive clit as she comes down.

There's no way I could ever walk away from this. Now that I've tasted her again, I know I will never want anything in my life more.

"You've come on my face twice now. I think that makes you mine."

"I'll be anything you want me to be if you promise to keep doing that."

Her breath is still coming in quick pants as she brushes her silky blonde hair out of her face.

I grab my belt, and with a loud thwack, pull it one-handed through the loops.

"Fuck, that's hot," she says, her eyes raking down my chest and torso. Having this beautiful woman check me out makes me grateful for all the hard work I put in at the gym.

Before I take off anything else, I pull out my wallet and toss it to her, then stand and pull off my pants.

"I'm not cheap. Are you sure you can afford me?" she says, holding up my wallet, and I stumble, nearly tripping over my pants as I remove my shoes and kick them the rest of the way off.

"That's not what…I'm not…" I splutter as I try to regain my composure, physically and mentally.

"Oh my God, I'm just fucking with you. You should see your face. Obviously, your first time is free," she says with a wink as she pulls the condom out, holding it between two fingers as she tosses my wallet onto my discarded clothes.

"I'm not sure if you're kidding," I say nervously as I stand before her naked.

"I should be paying you, 'cause *damn*, that dick," she says, stroking a finger up it as she traces the thick vein that wraps around my shaft.

She slowly lowers her mouth and licks around the crown of my cock, and my hips buck involuntarily in response.

"Mmm, this cock tastes like mine. I could lick your cum all day."

"I'd really, really fucking like that." I groan as she takes me to the back of her throat, bobbing and sucking as she works me over. Fuck, I'm totally going to come if she doesn't stop. My orgasm is building at the base of my spine, and it pains me to pull her off my cock. Not being inside this woman physically hurts.

"There will be time for soft and tender later. Right now, I need to fuck this perfect pink pussy. You've already come on my face and hand, now I want to cover my cock in your cum. Turn around, get on your knees, and grab the back of that throne," I growl as I take the condom from her hand, rip open the foil, and sheathe my dick.

She turns around and kneels on the plush seat pushing her ass toward me as she grips the chair. "Spank me, Daddy. I've been naughty," she says, wiggling her ass back and forth. I'm not sure if she's kidding or not, but I grip her hip in one hand and bring the other down on her right cheek, the crack echoing in the open space.

"Oh fuck," she moans, dropping her head.

"Such a naughty girl." I spank her other cheek hard and then cup it, smoothing away the sting.

Gripping the base of my shaft, I line it up with her opening, gliding the tip through her wetness as I tease her clit. The way her hips grind on me in response has my heart beating wildly in my chest. She wants this as much as I do, and fuck, I want this more than flames long for oxygen. I'm trembling and insatiable as I devour every inch of her exposed skin I can reach.

Thrusting into her feels like coming home. There's something familiar about the way we fit, but also new and exciting. It's open, raw, honest. There are no pretenses or formalities. Bella knows what she wants and goes after it, and it's unlike anything I've ever experienced in a partner.

She drops her head as she arches her ass, pushing back into

me as I grip her hips and set a steady rhythm. I'm not gentle. This is years of pent-up sexual energy and weeks of frustration releasing with each brutal thrust.

"Oh fuck, you feel so good. Is that all you got?"

"Can you handle more?"

"I need you to fuck me hard. Pull my hair. Grab my throat. Make me feel you for days. Don't hold back."

Gathering up the hair at the base of her neck, I give it a tug, forcing her face to mine as I kiss her hard. When I pull back, I lick along the shell of her ear as my hand slides down below her jaw to grip the slender column of her neck. "I'm going to embarrass myself with how quickly you're going to make me come. But don't for a second think that this is the only time I'm going to be inside this perfect cunt today. I can't get enough of you."

I gently squeeze the sides of her neck as I rut harder into her, reaching my other hand down to pinch her clit.

"Yes! Oh shit, fuck, right there, oh my God, right there. I'm going to. Oh fuck—" she moans, and I can feel a rush of liquid coat my hand as my release hits me and my thrusts get erratic before I still inside of her, filling up the condom.

My heart is racing as I pant for breath, gliding my soaked hand up her abdomen to pull her body flush with mine.

"That was incredible. I've never experienced anything like that." I kiss along her shoulder as she stretches an arm back and pulls my face to hers. It's an awkward angle, but the kiss lights a fire in me, coursing through every nerve ending in my body. I'm in awe of her, the way she touches me, responds to me, asks for exactly what she wants. It's everything I've ever wanted in a woman that I've never been able to vocalize.

When she pulls back, I stare into her grey-blue eyes, feeling seen, feeling wanted, her desire evident on her face. Reluctantly, I pull out of her and remove the condom, tying it off and throwing it in the garbage can nearby.

"Oh my God," she says, her voice sounding panicked as

she looks down at the throne. "I squirted all over Santa's chair!"

I can't help it. I throw my head back in laughter. It's probably a dick move—she looks genuinely horrified—but I can't hold it in.

"This isn't funny, Hardy. What if I ruined the chair?" she says as she starts pacing. "Amber is going to have a field day with this. She'll probably kick me out of the PTO."

"No one is getting kicked out of anything. I'm sure we can clean it."

"How? It's not like we can take it to a dry cleaner!" She's still pacing, and I grab her, pulling her into me as I stroke her back. "How do I always fuck things up?"

"You didn't fuck anything up. You're the farthest thing from a fuckup. You're a great mom, a wonderful teacher, and the best Christmas coach I've ever had."

"I'm the only Christmas coach you've ever had."

"Seriously, Bella, you're incredible. There's no way I could do everything you do, but you inspire me to try. I could never repay you for the things you've done to make this holiday a memorable one for Avery and me."

"You're pretty incredible yourself. Most guys I know wouldn't jump through all these hoops just to keep Santa alive for their kid."

Our eyes lock as I run a hand up her spine, relishing the way she shudders at my touch.

"But I seriously made a mess on that chair. Amber's going to tell everyone I screwed up again."

"So what if the mean girl that runs the PTO thinks you're a screwup? I know you're not, and so does everyone else that matters." I kiss her forehead and breathe in her soft minty scent. She's already helped me so much. I'm determined to show her how amazing she is, regardless of what Amber thinks.

"What's left on our list? Just the shopping and wrapping,

right?" She nods against my chest. "Perfect. I'm taking you out shopping. You can drag me anywhere you want, and I won't complain. And it's on me. You've done so much, it's my turn to take care of you."

"You don't have to do that."

"It's my turn now. If you weren't here, I'd have to do it on my own. But I'm very glad you are here. I can't imagine doing this with anyone else," I say, kissing her forehead.

CHAPTER 18
BELLA

We're in Hardy's truck headed for Denver, and I cannot stop thinking about the things this man did to my body. It was everything I was looking for the night we met; I just didn't realize then that I was with the wrong man. But if it hadn't been for that coward Brody calling 911, I wouldn't have had this mind-blowing experience with Hardy. How perfect he felt thrusting inside of me, the rough way he manhandled me exactly how I like, and the way he made me come on that chair.

Oh fuck, the chair.

"We should pick up some cleaner while we're out," I say.

He just shakes his head and smirks. "We got this," he says, reaching over to squeeze my thigh.

I place a hand on top of his, forcing him to leave it there. "We? Is there a we now? Are you finally ready to admit that I wore you down?" I wiggle my eyebrows.

"I tried to fight it, but it's useless. I'm drawn to you. Your humor, your heart, your…"

"Hot pocket?" I offer.

His laughter is infectious. "Hot pocket?"

"You had a whole H theme going there, I figured you were looking for another word for my lady parts."

"You've got a great one. Best I've ever had, but I'm not really into reducing women to their reproductive organs despite the dirty shit that comes out of my mouth in the moment. There's so much more to you than really good sex."

"I think that's the nicest thing a man has ever said to me," I admit softly. Why is my voice so quiet? Am I going to cry? Holy shit, I'm going to cry.

"That's the bare minimum, Bella. What kind of fuckwads have you been with that don't recognize how incredible you are? Actually, don't answer that. It doesn't matter who treated you badly before me. I'm here now, and I'm going to try my best to give you everything you deserve."

A small sniffle escapes despite my best effort to contain it, and I blink rapidly as I try to hold in the rest. I can feel Hardy's eyes on me, and he squeezes my thigh in silent support.

"I don't think you understand how much I needed to hear that. I've always been treated as an afterthought by the men in my life. It's probably why I use humor as a defense mecha-nism. They can't laugh at you if you laugh at yourself first."

"I know that you don't need a man in your life. But I hope that if you allow me to be in yours, it's because you chose me. I want to be the person you choose."

"Not that I'm not loving this road trip confession, but what changed? I feel like you were so hot and cold the past week."

"I talked to Avery this morning, and she not only gave me the girlfriend green light, but she also picked you specifically to be my girlfriend."

My head whips in his direction, trying to determine if he's kidding. "So, we can make it official?"

"I'm pretty sure we already have with as much time as we've been spending together. And I don't know if Ned's a big gossip or not, but you totally moaned right before he knocked.

I'm pretty sure he knew what we were up to on the other side of the door."

Letting go of his grip on my leg, I bury my head in my hands. "He's the worst. The whole town will know by the time we get home."

Just then, my phone buzzes in my coat pocket, and I fish it out.

AUNT DELILAH

Heard you and a certain firefighter finally bumped uglies

Oh my God, how did you know that? It literally just happened

"What was that gasp about?" Hardy asks, his gaze fixed on the road as we approach Denver traffic.

"My aunt just asked me if we fucked."

He coughs, pounding on his chest to clear it. "I'm sorry, what? Your aunt?"

"Yeah, Principal Adams."

"Your aunt is the principal?" It's kinda cute how high his voice gets when he's surprised.

"She's not technically my aunt."

He looks confused. "Didn't you just refer to her as your aunt?"

"She's like an aunt. She and my mom were best friends, and even though I was eighteen when she died, Delilah practically raised me after that."

My phone buzzes again.

Just heard a rumor from Ned that Hardy was at your house, but you confirmed the boinking 😉

"Shit. How could I fall for that?" I mumble to myself.

"Fall for what? I need you to fill in more details here," he says, turning on his blinker as we pull into the parking lot of a strip mall.

"Ned already ran his big mouth and Delilah just texted."

"Why does my daughter's principal want to know if we hooked up? Did Ned tell her we did?"

"Delilah kinda led me to believe that she knew we hooked up and then I accidentally admitted it. But it's okay. She already gave me the go-ahead."

He drops his head onto the steering wheel. "I will never get used to this, will I? How all up in your business small towns can be?"

"It grows on you."

An hour later we're walking through the aisle of a large retail store, looking for items for Avery.

I grab a Santa hat with a bell on the end and place it on Hardy's head. Which is not an easy feat given he's so much taller than me.

"Maybe you could wear that later for round two?" I say against his ear.

"Is that the last item from your text thread? Santa okay finger pointing at sparkly nuts?"

I place a hand on my heart. "Ah, you remembered. And I totally plan to bang you in the whole suit, I've just had trouble finding one in your size."

"Given the order of those texts, it would seem that Santa was pointing at the nuts, so I think you should wear the hat since I have the nuts." He places the hat on my head.

"Oh, I'm down for that too. Just not in the chair. It needs to dry after we clean it."

We stop in the cleaning aisle, deciding a bottle of upholstery cleaner will be our best bet, before heading to the toy aisle to grab the last of Avery's gifts.

"What did Isaac say Avery wanted from Santa?" he asks, as I look through the figurines, a cute pigeon set catching my eye.

"Lemme pull up my text thread with him." I scroll through

my phone until I find my thread with Isaac. "She told Isaac she wants some kind of sparkly princess castle."

"The ultimate sparkle princess palace with all the dolls you could ever want, batteries not included," he says like he's reciting straight from a commercial.

"That's the one, I think. She was kinda cryptic with Isaac."

"I think she has suspicions that I'm Santa and she's being vague on purpose because Santa would just know what she was talking about. Also, I remember her asking Lydie for that and her telling Avery that it was too expensive."

"So clearly Santa has to bring it if we want her to believe. Did you decide what Santa tier you want to do?"

"I honestly have no idea," he says, scratching his neck.

"What did Lydie used to do? We could aim to make it similar."

"She would pick a couple items off her list, but then she'd always throw in something extra, something Avery didn't ask for specifically but would absolutely love. But it was never anything as big as what she's asking for this year. Can I do that?"

"The beauty of The Santa Rules is you can change tiers at any time. You can do it if your kids are misbehaving, or if your financial situation changes, or your beliefs. Anything really. We could stick to something close to what Lydie did and slowly add to or subtract from it over time. But if Avery's asking Santa for something big, you could put her on that tier for this year and then talk to her later if you decide you want Santa to bring smaller or cheaper items. Later you can reframe it to shift the focus off getting big ticket items."

"Won't that make her suspicious?"

"Not if you say something like, 'We're fortunate to be able to buy our own gifts for each other and we don't need Santa to bring us as much, so we opted into a different tier.' This way, Santa still brings a gift, but the emphasis isn't on all the stuff Santa can bring her. You can frame it like Santa is really busy too, and the less he brings us, the quicker he can deliver all the presents, and we want to make sure everyone gets a gift to open on Christmas."

"What did you do?"

"Well, I wanted credit for the gifts I bought Isaac, but Jake would always throw money at him. We were on a high tier when we were married, but after the divorce, I had to explain that each parent can decide what they want Santa to bring into their own houses. Honestly, it saved my ass and bought me another year of him believing. And I used The Santa Rules to explain why his Christmas looked different at his dad's. I just told him his dad was still learning how to use the app. And I moved to a different tier since my new house was smaller, and I didn't have room for too much, since I knew his dad would still buy him tons of shit."

Hardy locates the sparkly palace amid a sea of pink and adds it to the cart. "I think this is my only option this year, but I like what you said about focusing more on giving back to others and only getting something small from Santa."

We walk through another aisle, and Hardy tosses a few blind bags into the cart.

"Oh, I love those! Really gets the blood flowing when you don't know what's inside. But once you rip that thing open and see that it's the rare collectable you're missing? BAM! Dopamine!"

He holds up the blind bag, a smirk curling one side of his face. "You mean these *kids'* toys?"

"They bring me joy," I say as he leans into me and I boop him on the nose.

His warm hand wraps around my waist as he leans in to kiss me. The feel of his lips on mine sends a wave of lust coursing through my body as I slide a hand up his chest to hold his face.

A throat clears behind us, and we break apart, moving out

of the way for the impatient person walking by when I hear a familiar judgy, nasal voice.

"Bella? Funny seeing you here. With your student's parent. Sucking face in the toy aisle." Amber's arms are crossed, an eyebrow raised as she looks me up and down, disdain dripping in her tone.

I feel Hardy's body tense as he takes a step toward her, but I tug him back, stepping in front of him and pulling his arms around me like we're posing for a prom photo.

"Amber. I would say it's nice to see you, but it's not."

"Babe," a voice slurs from behind her, and I see Chuck walking up.

Hardy's grip on me tightens as Chuck's eyes look me over from head to toe. "Bella, what a pleasant surprise."

I wish I could say the same, but his attention creeps me out. I don't know what Amber sees in him, and I have no clue what teenage me saw in him, but I made a lot of mistakes after my mom died when I was trying to grieve and figure out who I was.

Amber looks between us and slaps Chuck in the gut. She turns back to me and props her hand on her hip, flicking the hair from her ponytail off her collar. "Shouldn't you two be working on the workshop?"

"Just picking up some last-minute items." It's not technically a lie. "We really should be going." I thread a hand through Hardy's as I lead us away from them. I don't have to look back to know he's giving Chuck some serious side-eye as we pass.

We quickly head to the checkout, and at Hardy's request, I grab some sodas for the road while he starts scanning items in self-checkout. After we load everything into the back of his truck, I climb in the cab and wait for him to return the cart. As soon as his ass hits the seat and he closes his door, he turns to me right as I'm tugging his collar.

With our noses pressed against the other's, he smiles against my lips. "Guess we had the same idea."

I nod as he presses his lips to mine and steals the breath from my lungs. The kiss is deep and slow as he takes his time exploring my mouth. His hands are gentle, holding my face as if it's the most precious thing to him.

I let out a sigh when he pulls back. "What was that for?"

His penetrating gaze is intense as he stares at me with so much longing, I can't help but look away, trying to gather my thoughts. Hands still on my cheeks, he tilts my head up, forcing me to look at him, but he doesn't say anything, not with his mouth anyway. His eyes are a different story. It's as though he's trying to process a lifetime of feelings, willing me to see the rawest part of who he is. And even though he doesn't answer my question with words, I can almost hear his thoughts as his eyes continue to shift between mine, like he's unsure which one to focus on because he's too close.

You matter to me.

I will protect you.

I'm falling for you.

Oh shit, does he love me? Do I love him?

A loud knock at the window startles us. We look over to find Chuck leering, giving us a thumbs-up that feels like a cheap assessment of a moment that's entirely too big to explain with words.

"I hate that guy," Hardy mutters out of the side of his mouth.

"I know you do," I say, grabbing his cheek to shift his focus back to me. "Thank you."

His brows pinch in confusion. "For what?"

"For letting me fight my own battle in there. I could feel the anger and tension in your body. Most guys would have gone all alpha on him and gotten in his face. And younger me would have thrived off that. But now that I'm older and wiser,

I can pick my own battles, and I appreciate your silent support."

"I've known a lot of guys like him. Running his mouth, looking for a fight. But I have a little girl to look out for, and I'm all she has. If I lose my temper and punch him, she suffers while I go to jail. He's not worth losing her over. And after you told me how you handed Amber her ass the other day, I was kinda hoping for my own front-row seat for round two."

I pull him in for another kiss, and there's another knock on the window as Chuck makes a finger-in-the-hole gesture followed by another thumbs-up.

"Okay, I need to get away from this douche canoe. I only have so much self-control."

"Agreed."

CHAPTER 19
BELLA

We get everything unloaded from the truck and into the house, and Hardy helps me carry down all the wrapping supplies from my closet. I didn't even try to jump his bones when we were in my bedroom, and I'm proud of myself for that. Hardy, on the other hand, keeps checking me out, and I catch him readjust himself every chance he gets.

Laying out all the supplies on the kitchen table, I ask the hard-hitting question. "Ribbon or bows?"

"There is nothing I'd love more than to see you wrapped up in this and nothing else," he says, holding up a spool of ribbon. "Actually, this gives me an idea."

"I love where your mind is headed, but we have to wrap these gifts first or we'll never finish."

"Oh, I'll make sure we both finish."

I throw my head back in laughter. "I love this side of you," I say, cringing at the fact that I keep saying love, especially after that moment we shared in the parking lot earlier.

"And I love…" he trails off, and his almost confession hangs heavy in the air between us as he eyes my lips.

Is it too soon to feel this strongly about him? Could I love him already?

"I love this. Spending time with you. And not just you—all of us, Isaac and Avery too. It feels like a little piece of my soul heals every time we're all together. Like I was meant to find you on that call that night so you could be a part of my life, our lives."

He moves around the table, gathering me in his arms as he pulls me tightly against him. I can feel his heart beating wildly in his chest and it comforts me knowing that I might not be alone in this feeling.

"I'm so thankful you're helping make Christmas special for us. You don't know how much this means to me."

Then his lips are on mine and all my resolve goes out the window as he lifts me into his arms, grabs the spool of ribbon, and carries me up to my bedroom. My arms rub up and down his thick biceps as I wrap my legs around his waist.

When he sets me on the edge of the bed, he pulls his shirt off, exposing his sculpted abs and the slutty little V lines that disappear into his pants. I can't help but trace one with my finger as he pulls his pants and boxers off and then helps me take off my clothes as well. The only piece of clothing remaining is the Santa hat on my head just like he promised.

There's no slow striptease when you're a parent. It's a race to get naked so you can spend the bulk of your time exploring each other. And do we ever.

He grabs the ribbon, pulling a section of it free as he holds my hands in one of his and winds the red satin around my wrists. There's just enough left on the spool to bind my hands but nothing else.

With a single hand, he gently pushes me back against the mattress. "One day, I'm going to bind your entire body in ribbon, or rope."

My breath hitches in my throat at his promise as my chest expands against his palm.

"Would you like that? Being covered in my knots? Restrained so I can have total control over your pleasure?"

All words escape me as his words play out in my mind like a wonderfully dirty movie, and I nod.

He slowly leans down, trailing a tongue around my nipple while his hand pinches the other, squeezing it between two fingers. Every nerve in my body is on fire as he pulls my nipple into his mouth and flicks it rapidly with his tongue.

"Holy fuck!" I moan as he somehow manages to flick it faster while rolling the other with his fingers. I can feel his hard length against my thigh, and I try to move my hips to position his cock against me, but I can't with the way he has me pinned down, so I settle for humping against his leg like a dog in heat. I'm so desperate for release, I'm practically begging. "Fuck, Hardy, please keep doing that. Please."

And he does. This man doesn't say a word, doesn't nod, he just keeps flicking his tongue as I shamelessly grind my pussy against his thigh. Between the pinching, humping, and the otherworldly flicking, I feel the early tingle of my orgasm build and I let out a low moan when he abruptly pulls back.

"You don't come until I say you can come. Nod if you understand."

I quickly nod, overcome with lust at the feral look in his eyes.

"This pussy is mine. Mine to eat. Mine to tease. Mine to fuck. Mine."

Okay, I love this side of him. There is nothing hotter than a man who knows what he wants in the bedroom. Who isn't afraid to boss me around and bend me to his will.

He pushes off the bed, grips my thighs, and pulls me to the edge as he kneels. God, this man really does like eating pussy.

"I want you to wrap your legs around my head so tight you worry about my ability to take in oxygen. I want you to smother me in your arousal until it's all I can breathe, all I can smell, and all I can taste."

When he presses his face to my pussy, he teases my lips until I'm so wet, so desperate to have him touch my clit that

I'm bucking frantically against him. Placing his arm over my lower abdomen, he holds me in place, forcing me to endure his teasing torture as he pushes his tongue into my opening, swirling it all the way around before thrusting it in and out.

My legs are limp on his shoulder when it hits me that I'm not following his directions, so I wrap them around his head, using my calves to guide him further up my pussy. And he goes willingly, lapping at my clit like it's his last meal and he hasn't eaten in days.

Every color of the rainbow flashes behind my eyelids when I pinch them shut, reveling in the sensation of his tongue against me. He slides his huge palms up my thighs and under my ass, gripping my cheeks as he buries himself further against me. I'm so close, so damn close as I press my thighs into the sides of his face and try to grip the comforter with my bound hands.

Right as I'm about to come, he pries my thighs open and pushes off the bed, standing back from it as he inhales deep breaths.

How? How does he know each time I'm about to come? I let out a frustrated sigh as he takes a step toward me.

"Do you see what you do to me?" he asks, fisting his cock, and I watch as he swipes his thumb over the tip, collecting the precum there. "Taste the mess you make of me."

He climbs onto the mattress, straddling me as he grips my jaw and forces it open, pushing his thumb inside as I suck it clean.

"Now taste the mess I make of you," he commands as he lowers his face to mine and thrusts his tongue in my mouth. The tangy taste of my arousal hits my tongue and ignites a frenzy in both of us as I place my bound wrists around his neck and pull him closer to me.

When he rolls onto his back, pulling me on top of him, I move down his body, grinding against his cock proudly reaching up his stomach. His hands grip my hips, halting my movement. "Condom."

"I'm on the pill, and my last test was clear."

"I asked for an STI screening at my physical last week, but I haven't been with anyone else in years."

"Are you telling me I can ride this fat cock bare?"

"Fuck, you can't talk to me like that right now, or I'm going to come in two pumps."

"Then fill me up and fuck me so hard that all the dirty thoughts escape me, and all I can do is moan."

He lifts my hips and guides me onto his cock, pulling me down inch by inch. He thrusts slowly, letting me adjust to his size, and I lean against his chest, my bound hands stacked one on the other as I grip him to steady myself.

This new position feels incredible. Normally I prefer doggie style, but he has the perfect length and girth that each thrust hits a spot deep inside me that has me on the edge already.

His grip on my hips tightens as he starts fucking up into me, making the bells on my Santa hat jingle with each snap of his hips.

"Oh fuck, this cunt feels so fucking perfect. So fucking mine." His pace increases as he reaches down to pinch my clit.

And then I'm free-falling over the edge into a bliss so deep and so wide, I feel like I'm drowning in an endless abyss of pleasure.

"That's it, Bells. Squeeze this cock, milk me for every drop of my cum. It's yours. Fuck, it's yours," he growls as his movements get sloppy and he stills inside of me, and I feel a rush of warmth as he fills me with his cum. I collapse onto his chest, our breathing in sync as we cling to each other.

"Bells? Where did that come from?" I say, popping my head up and arching an eyebrow.

"I dunno. I think I was starting to say Bella and then I kept hearing those bells each time I thrusted into you, and it just came out."

"Is it weird that I like it?" I say as I gingerly slide off his body, rolling onto my side next to him.

I watch as he looks down at his cock and fists it, collecting the cum that leaked onto him. Then he rolls me to my back, pushes my legs open, and slaps my pussy hard, rubbing the mess we made around my opening before pushing it back inside as I gasp.

"You forgot something, Bells. This cunt is mine. And I want it full of my cum. We're going to go back downstairs and wrap those presents. And I want to do so knowing that you're so full of me it's dripping from you."

The mouth on this man. "Now this is a Christmas tradition I can get behind."

CHAPTER 20
HARDY

A switch has flipped inside me. After my talk with Avery this morning, I've been consumed with thoughts of Bella. Everything I've been holding in for weeks has suddenly come bubbling to the surface the same way a soda fizzes and overflows when you fill the cup up too quickly. It's messy and raw, and I'm scared as fuck, but there's something in her eyes that tells me that we're going to be okay. That moment in the truck—when we stared into each other's eyes—was a turning point for me.

Something about the way that Chuck guy looked at her and the way Amber spoke to her had warning bells going off in my head. It's not the same kind of danger I feel when I arrive on the scene of a fire, but it told me that Bella wasn't entirely safe. I realize there is nothing I can do to shelter her from the hurtful words or lustful gaze of others, but I want to protect her the same way I want to protect Avery. Like she's already part of my heart, part of my family.

And I almost told her. But like a fucking coward, I chickened out. So I forced her to see the sincerity in my eyes, to feel the longing in my touch. If I couldn't say the words yet, I wanted her to know how I felt in other ways.

Until that asshole kept knocking on our window, ruining the moment.

Now she's sitting across from me at the kitchen table, squirming in her seat as she shows me how to crease the paper just the right way so it doesn't wrinkle. And all I can think about is that crease between her legs stuffed full of my cum. She keeps biting her lower lip each time she leans forward, and it makes my dick twitch.

I'm in my mid-thirties and I've already fucked this woman twice today, yet I feel like I could go another round and still not get enough of her. And part of me wants to take advantage of this time alone because who knows when we'll get another opportunity like this again? I can't keep leaving Avery with Maggie when I promised not to give up any more time with her. I already feel guilty about that, but I could justify it because these Santa lessons are for her. But I don't want Avery to feel like I'm choosing someone over her. I would choose them both. And Isaac too.

We empty all the bags we bought today, and when I look at the pile of stocking stuffers, it looks too small in comparison to how big I picture her stocking in my head.

"I might need to get Avery a few more things. I'm not sure that small pile will fill her stocking."

"Stocking stuffing is a science, but I always recommend erring on the side of too much. Then anything that doesn't fit can go under the tree. But don't worry, I got you covered," she says, as she walks over to a closet and pulls out several bags with little books and trinkets.

These are perfect for Avery, and I'm blown away by how well Bella has figured out my little girl. "How?"

She shrugs. "I saw her eyeing things when we were out the other night with Isaac."

"But she was with you."

"Such a man thing to say. Moms have perfected the art of

buying their kids gifts under their noses for years. I could coach you on it, but I don't think it's a skill you'd master."

I bite my lower lip and smile when her phone lights up on the table. We sit in silence as I wrap the last of Avery's gifts, agonizing over my abysmal creases. Bella has delicate fingers, but mine are too thick and clumsy to fold the paper neatly on such tiny gifts. When I hear Bella laugh, I look up, expecting her to tease me for my shitty wrapping, but she's still staring at her phone.

"What's so funny?" I ask, nodding at her phone.

"Nothing, just cookie porn." She says it so casually like I'm supposed to know what the hell she's talking about. I blink, waiting for her to explain.

She tilts the phone toward me showing off a picture of an older woman biting into a cookie that looks like an elephant trunk, but something is off about the shape. "Is that Principal Adams?" I take the phone from her to zoom in on the cookie.

"Is that an elephant trunk cookie in her hand?"

"Looks like it." She laughs like there's more to the story that she's not telling me.

"What's cookie porn?"

"It's just pictures of cookies we send each other. You know, like food porn, but just cookies."

"Only cookies?" I ask incredulously.

"Only Cookies! Oh my God, that's genius. I have to text that to her," she says, snatching the phone back as she types furiously.

"I feel like I'm missing a punchline here."

"Only Cookies! Like Only Fans, but Only Cookies!"

The front door swings open, and I turn my head as Bella flings her body over the table, like she's trying to smother a fire.

"Oh good, your tits aren't out this time," Isaac says as he kicks off his shoes and walks toward us.

"What are you doing home? I thought you were at your dad's until tomorrow?" Bella asks, still lying on the table.

"Why are you on the table like that? Ew. Were you guys doing it?"

I hold up my hands like I'm innocent as Bella's protests fill the air. "What? No! We weren't doing anything inappropriate. We were wrapping gifts, and you scared me, so I flung myself over them to hide them from you," she says as she slowly pushes up. "But I already have your gifts wrapped, and you're clearly not Avery, so I don't know why I did that." She brushes several loose strands of hair out of her face.

"Methinks the lady doth protest too much." I laugh at my own joke, but Bella cocks her hip, placing a hand on it.

"Whose side are you on, buddy?"

"I like him," Isaac says, offering me a fist bump as he walks to the fridge. His head pops out for a second as he looks at me. "But only if you promise to never talk about banging my mom." And then his head is buried in the fridge again.

Bella props a hand on her hip. "So, not that I'm not thrilled that you're here, but why are you here? Everything okay with your dad?"

He shrugs and his eyes flick to me. I get a sinking feeling in my gut at the way he's looking at me, like he's trying to tell me something with his eyes that he doesn't want Bella to know.

"It's whatever." He grabs an apple and bites into it as he surveys the mess we've made on the table. "Are you done wrapping?"

"I think so." She gathers up several empty wrapping tubes in her arms. "I'm gonna toss these in the bin outside before one of you starts a sword fight."

Damn, I was totally going to swat her with one of those. Once the door closes behind her, I round on Isaac.

"What's going on with your dad?"

He rolls his eyes. "He wasn't home. Well, he was when Mom dropped me off, but once his girlfriend showed up, they went out to dinner, so I got a friend to pick me up and bring me home."

"Does your dad know you left?"

He won't look at me. "Probably not."

"Jesus, Isaac. You need to tell him, or your mom."

"Tell me what?" Bella says from the door, and we both jump. "Are the two of you keeping secrets from me?" Her tone is teasing as she walks in. "Oh, shit you are," she says with more of a bite.

I give him a look, and he lets out a sigh. "Dad doesn't know I left."

"And?" I prompt him.

"And he wasn't home when I left. Derek's mom picked me up and dropped me off over here."

Bella gives me a curious look, and the guilt slams into me.

Isaac sighs as he continues. "And this isn't the first time he's left me at the house. But I'm never technically alone there."

"Because he leaves his kid with his staff instead of actually spending time with him," she mutters, pacing the kitchen.

"Ever since he started dating Kelsey, he's never around anymore." He says it quietly, but I can hear the hurt in his tone.

Bella stops pacing and turns to him. "How long has this been going on, Isaac?"

"A few months."

"Is this why you don't want to spend Christmas out there?" she asks.

He looks at me, and I nod for him to tell her. "Yeah. I told Hardy last week." He gives me a small smile as Bella turns to me.

"You knew?"

"He asked me not to say anything. It wasn't technically neglect since he was never home alone but even then, there's no age limit in Colorado for when a kid can be left home alone.

It was really shitty of his dad to put him in that situation, but I figured as long as no laws were being broken, he'd tell you eventually."

"Are you mad?" Isaac asks, vulnerability in his tone.

She lets out a long exhale as she walks over to the sink and leans on it. "I am mad. But not at either of you." She turns to us, leaning against the edge of the counter. "While I love that you two are getting along, I don't like being left in the dark about this kind of stuff. But I'm also glad you have each other."

"I'm sorry," Isaac and I say in unison.

"You need to text your dad and let him know you left, and I pray I don't get an earful from him."

"But it was my choice. You didn't even know."

"Still." She nods at Isaac, then looks at me. "And you, I'll deal with later." There's a hint of a teasing tone in her voice.

"Please don't make me go back over there," Isaac begs.

"Since it's your dad's weekend, that's not up to me."

Isaac retreats upstairs, head buried in his phone. As soon as he's out of sight, Bella pulls me into a hug.

"Thank you."

"For what?" I ask, rubbing her back as she presses her cheek into my chest.

"For being a safe space for my kid. He and his dad don't always get along, and he doesn't share a lot with me, but he trusted you. And you kept his trust, even if I don't like it."

"I did do that, didn't I?"

These two have found a place in my heart in such a short amount of time. I've lived an entire lifetime without them, but suddenly I can't imagine not having them in my life, and I'm determined to figure out a way to keep them in it beyond Christmas.

CHAPTER 21
BELLA

It means a lot that someone loves my kid the way I love my kid. I just wished his dad loved him like that too.

Wait. Did I just say love? It feels like he loves us. Does he love us? Do I love him? I think I love him.

"Miss Carlisle, can I go to the potty?" Avery asks, pulling me out of my head. Focus, Bella. You are the adult. You have responsibilities. You can't keep daydreaming about the hot firefighter all day.

"Can you hold it for ten more minutes till we walk down to lunch?" I ask Avery.

She nods and skips back to her seat, and I get up from my desk to start corralling kids and cleaning up before we go to the cafeteria.

As we're walking down the hall, Lucy waves at me, and I walk over and lean against the wall next to her as our kids go in and out of the bathroom.

"What's with the face? Rough day?"

"No, just thinking about some stuff that I'm not ready to process out loud," I admit.

"About a certain widower that needs help with Christmas?"

"Maybe," I say right as Avery walks out of the bathroom and shuffles over to me.

"Are you coming to our house tonight?"

I can feel my cheeks turning red as I glance around. "Not tonight."

"Don't you need to work on the secret project?" she asks, whispering the last part.

"Actually, we are in a good spot with that. Your daddy got a lot of work done this weekend."

"Oh," she says, looking disappointed.

"I'm sure we'll work on it more later in the week, though. Why?"

"I like it when you come over. My daddy smiles more. I think he likes helping with the workshop."

"Oh, he likes something, alright," Lucy murmurs under her breath.

I jab an elbow against her side.

"Go get in line so we can go to lunch."

Avery skips over to her spot in line, and I do a quick count to see how many kids I'm waiting on.

"What's really going on with you two?" Lucy asks.

"What do you mean?"

"I know you're working on Santa's Workshop together, but are you sure that's it?"

I know the rumor mill is already running since we've been seen around town, but I suddenly feel guilty for keeping my friends in the dark. And Hardy and I haven't discussed if we were officially telling people about us, but Amber did see us kissing. And Avery is still in earshot and I'm not sure what she knows about me and her dad.

"He's helping me with the workshop, and I'm helping him with The Santa Rules," I say, lowering my voice, repeating the line I used on her the last time she asked this.

"Okaaaay," Lucy says, drawing out the word as though she doesn't believe me.

Lunch and recess pass too quickly, but luckily Lucy doesn't ask any more questions about Hardy.

There's a lively discussion in the afternoon as we practice working on our handwriting. When I ask for different words that start with S, the topic soon changes to Santa, and I decide it's a great opportunity to see if I can get Avery to open up about her favorite traditions.

I walk around the room and ask students what they like to do during the holidays, and it's always fascinating to hear everyone's plans. Not everyone celebrates Christmas, but most of the kids talk about hanging out with their family and playing with siblings and friends. Every so often I glance over at Avery, and she has her head down like she's concentrating on her writing extra hard.

When I walk over to her table, I squat next to her. "Those are some beautiful Ss." I point to her writing.

"Thanks."

"I didn't hear you share your favorite holiday traditions." I speak softly for only her to hear, not wanting to draw attention as the rest of the class works.

"My mommy used to sing all the songs. I liked that."

"What was your favorite?" I ask, hoping I can get her to share more, not just so I can help Hardy, but also so she knows that it's okay to share her big feelings.

"The under the tree one."

"Kelly Clarkson. I love that one. Did you two ever go caroling?"

"What's that?"

"It's when you walk around and sing Christmas songs. You can go door to door and spread Christmas cheer. Would you like to do that?"

She nods her head.

"Do you have any other fun traditions that your family does?"

"Cookies. But Daddy burned them last year, and Santa

threw them in the trash."

"Oh no. We will have to make sure that you have some good cookies for Santa this year, then."

"What's your favorite tradition?" she asks, finally looking up from her paper.

"My favorite is something cool Santa used to do for Isaac. He's too old for it now so I asked him to stop, but Santa used to leave him a paper wall to run through."

"That's so cool! How come Santa doesn't do that for me?"

"Well, there are certain rules that Santa has to follow."

"Because Daddy is the boss of our house?"

"That's right. And Santa can't just make a mess in your house without your daddy's approval."

"Is that why Sprinkle didn't come last year?"

"Maybe," I say, trying to stifle a laugh since I know exactly why her elf went missing. "There are Santa Rules. And if you want Santa to leave you a paper wall, you have to make sure your daddy opts into that with Santa, then Santa knows he has permission to leave one," I tell her quietly, making sure no other students hear.

Avery gets quiet like she's thinking over what else she could ask Santa for, so I push up and continue wandering the room. As I walk around my students, I devise my own plan for how I could bring more cheer to this little girl's holiday.

How good is your singing voice?

??

Never mind, it doesn't matter. Guess what we're doing tonight?

If the answer isn't your sweet cunt, then I don't want to hear it

That will require babysitters

And this won't?

Not tonight. Guess what we're doing?

It's a school night

So grumpy

Do you want to know what brings me joy?

I know what I want the answer to be

That does bring me joy, but I'm trying to coach you on Christmas stuff. Focus

Whatever we're doing, can it involve less glitter?

Wait, are we going caroling?

How did you know?

You asked if I could sing

Oh yeah, I did. And we are

I feel like you're about to quote that line from Elf about spreading cheer

I'm impressed you know an Elf reference

Avery made me watch it the other night. It made me think of you

I love that you know me so well

Shit. *Like*. I *like* that he knows me so well. My heart races in my chest as I wait for his reply, and I watch those three little dots dance with nervous anticipation.

> I have thoroughly enjoyed getting to know you

I breathe out a sigh of relief. That was a close one.

Three hours later, a grumpy, bundled-up Hardy is trudging toward me down the sidewalk, and I can't help the goofy grin that takes over my face when I see his appearance. Avery runs to me.

"Doesn't Daddy look pretty?"

"I thought we were doing less glitter this time?" I wave a hand in a circle around his face.

"Avery has always wanted me to grow a beard, but since the department has rules about the length of our facial hair, she rubbed glue on my face and gave me a beard with glitter."

"You look…very sparkly."

"It's itchy."

I lean in to give him a hug, savoring the smell of pine, smoke, and bergamot.

"She told me I needed to look pretty for my date," he says quietly into my ear.

"Oh, got a hot date after this?" I tease.

"Can we sing the songs now?" Avery says, running over to us as she tugs on Hardy's coat.

"So where are we doing this?" Hardy asks.

"I figured we'd walk through the local shops. See if we can get people to join our merry band."

"Daddy loves to sing," Avery says. "He practiced the whole way here."

"He did, did he?" Hardy's cheeks are pink, though that could just be the cold. Is he trying to impress me? "So, what's your favorite Christmas song?"

He starts to open his mouth, but Avery interrupts him. "He likes 'Silent Night.'"

"That's a good one," I agree. "Our first stop is Chestnut Roasters."

"Can we get a cookie too?" Avery asks, as she walks ahead of us.

"No Isaac?" Hardy asks, looking behind us.

"Nah, singing isn't his thing. He's gaming at a friend's house, said they were working on a coding thing or something. Plus, he was worried I'd change the lyrics of 'Twelve Days of Christmas' to 'Twelve Pubes a-Counting.' I did threaten it, so I guess I don't blame him."

"Twelve what? Wait, never mind. You'd think I'd have learned by now not to question you."

"I'll tell you later," I say, right as Avery catches up to us and grabs Hardy's hand.

The delicious aroma of coffee and sugar has me doing a little dance as we walk in.

"What was that?" Hardy smirks.

"I'm just excited."

"Can we get hot chocolate?" Avery asks, bouncing on the balls of her feet.

"Sweet Jesus, there are two of them," Hardy teases, glancing between us.

After two hot chocolates, three cookies, one with glitter sprinkles for Avery, and way too many napkins, we head out of the store, fueled up on sugar and ready to start caroling at our next stop: Chestnut Mountain Market.

I suddenly trip over a crack in the sidewalk. "Oh crap," I yelp, nearly twisting my ankle as I throw my hands out to catch my fall. Before I hit the concrete, large hands grip my waist, steadying me.

"Careful, Bells. I got you."

I look down at my boot and notice the heel has separated from the sole. I try to take another step on it and wobble again.

"I have a better idea," Hardy says as he moves in front of me and squats down. "Hop on."

"Are you sure? We have like three more stops."

"It would be my honor," he says, smiling at me over his shoulder then motions for me to get on his back.

I climb on, wrapping my legs around his waist. Jake never would've carried me; he would have criticized me for my choice in footwear instead. But Hardy is a rock, someone steady and calm to depend on. And it feels good to know that I'm not alone, that I have someone else I can literally lean on.

We get about ten steps down the street when it hits me. "Hardy! Do you know what I am right now?"

He chuckles. "No, but I bet you're gonna tell me."

"Well, you've heard of Elf on the Shelf? I'm Bella on her fella!" I say and revel in his warmth as I feel laughter reverberate through his chest.

"That you are, Bells. I'm honored to be your fella."

We step inside the market, and Avery holds the door for us. "I want a piggyback ride too!"

"Miss Carlisle broke her shoe," Hardy explains as I climb down his back.

"It's okay, I can stand in here if she wants a turn."

Avery squeals as Hardy leans down and grabs her, placing her on his shoulders.

"Are you ready?" I ask Avery.

"Yup!"

"What should we sing?" I ask, but before anyone can answer, Hardy winks at me.

"Silent Night, holy night, all is calm, all is bright." His voice is soft yet powerful, his tone surprisingly velvety.

I think my ovaries just melted. Just when I think this man couldn't get any hotter, he has to have a voice like that. And not only does he sound great, but the fact that this grumpy man, who isn't a fan of crowds, is willing to do this for his daughter? I couldn't swoon harder. If I'm not careful, he's going to notice the little cartoon heart bubbles coming out of my eyes.

"Sleep in heavenly peace," Avery chimes in with her sweet little voice.

"Sleep in heavenly peace," I sing with them.

A few shoppers stop and listen as we sing several other songs, and a handful of people sing along with us. We stop at two other stores on Main Street, and each time, Hardy carries me outside and lets Avery sit on his shoulders while we sing.

And for the first time in a long time, my heart feels full. Being a mom has always fulfilled me, and I wish Isaac were with us tonight, but when I'm with these two people, I get the same feeling I do when I'm with my son. It feels soothing, like a warm mug of hot chocolate, familiar like coming home after a long trip, and it feels like love, the kind you feel on Christmas morning when you watch your kid open presents and see pure joy on their face, knowing that you were a part of that.

"Can we make cookies now?" Avery asks as we load her up in the car.

"Actually, we are making cookies this Sunday at Principal Delilah's house," I say.

"Can we come? Please?" Avery begs as Hardy shoots me an apologetic look.

"You can absolutely come." The thought of sharing this tradition with them warms my heart.

I just hope I don't scare Hardy off once he sees what kind of cookies we make.

CHAPTER 22
BELLA

"Are you coming tonight?" Lucy yells across the gym.

Hardy's head pops out from behind a piece of scenery, and he looks at me in confusion. "Do you have plans tonight?" He almost sounds hurt.

"I thought we were painting tonight," Avery says, running over.

Lucy walks toward us, checking out the progress we're making as Isaac stands on top of a ladder, earbuds in as he paints. "Sorry, I didn't know you had plans. It looks great," she says, pointing to the flats that are nearly finished.

"We only have a little bit more to do. Maybe another hour or two of work, depending on how the little one holds out," I say, setting my paintbrush down.

"So, you're not coming? It's okay, I can tell the girls. I mean, this will be the first time in seven years you haven't made it to the ugly sweater party, but I'm sure they'll be cool with it even if they were hoping to see Hardy too."

"Shoot, that totally slipped my mind. But way to lay on the guilt, Lucy."

"We got this, if you want to go," Hardy says reluctantly.

"Can I go?" Avery begs.

"Actually, it's kind of a grown-up-only party," I explain.

"But I don't want you to go. I want you to stay and help with the glitter."

I give Lucy an apologetic look, and she winks at me then glances at Hardy. "I'll let the girls know you can't make it." She walks out, and I turn back to my flat, picking up my brush and dipping it in the paint when Hardy walks over.

"Avery goes to bed at eight."

"Seems like a reasonable bedtime for a six-year-old, but it's not a school night. You could live a little, Hardy."

He lowers his voice. "What I'm saying is I won't miss any time with Avery if we go after she's asleep. Maggie can come over in case she wakes up, and we can have grown-up time."

"Oh? Oh!"

"I swear to everything holy, if I can't taste you tonight, I'm going to lose my mind."

"Well, we wouldn't want that," I say, a smile crooking one side of my face as I try to pretend that I'm only interested in what I'm painting in front of me. When now, all I can think about is his mouth on me teasing, his hands groping me and spanking me while he fills me up with his fat cock.

"Your ears turn red when you're horny too," he whispers.

I grab one, attempting to hide it from him. "They do not!"

"You're right, they don't. But now I know you're horny too."

My head falls back in laughter as he walks over to help Avery with her painting. For the next two hours, he's a man on a mission, working on overdrive to get things done so we can get Avery to bed and have a parents' night out.

I text the girls that I'm coming to the party late, and Hardy and I decide to have him pick me up once Avery's asleep.

My sweet neighbor Cora agreed to hang out at the house with Isaac so he won't be alone, and she's fixing herself a cup of decaf when Hardy knocks on the door. I thank her again and grab the box I made for Hardy.

When I open the door, I can't help but take him in from head to toe. He is easily the most attractive man I've ever seen. "You're not wearing an ugly sweater."

"This is the first Christmas season that I haven't lived in a firehouse, so my wardrobe choices are limited."

"You have two options: We can stop and get you a sweater, or you can carry this around all night." I hold up a square white box, wrapped up with a beautiful red bow.

"Since we aren't going to be at this party for long, I'll take the box."

"An excellent choice."

"Why do I feel like I'm going to regret this?" he says, examining the package. "And what is this hole for?" He shakes the box, and it starts vibrating.

"Since you don't have an ugly sweater—and trust me, you don't want to show up without one—I made you a makeshift costume. All you have to do is hold that box in front of your crotch."

He lifts the corner to peek inside. "Is this what I think it is?"

"It's a dick in a box! Like the SNL skit. Well, it's a vibe in a box. I didn't think you'd want to put your actual dick in a box."

"It's purple. People are going to think that I have an alien dick."

"Oh no, those have way more tentacles and doodads according to some books I've read."

"What?" he asks, looking like he's seen a ghost.

"Don't worry about it."

He holds up the vibrator in one hand, easily covering most of it with his large palm. "It's kinda small, don't you think?"

"That's actually pretty average. You, sir, are larger than most."

"Can't say I don't love hearing that."

"Don't act like you don't know you have a big dick."

His smile is wolfish as his eyes take in my outfit.

"Does that say you're an expert ball handler?"

I grin, pulling the sweater tight across my chest so he can see the hands cupping the ornament balls that are strategically placed to look like they're holding my tits.

"That's fantastic."

"You have the cock, and I handle balls."

"We're a match made in tacky Christmas sweater heaven," he says as we head to his truck. He opens the door for me and looks back at the house. "You know, I'm kind of surprised you don't have more lights up."

"That would require dangling from a ladder, and as we all know, I should not be trusted with those. Projector lights and inflatables are my safest options."

"Maybe I could hang some lights for you next year," he offers as he climbs into the driver's seat.

My heart does a little fluttery dance in my chest. Is this man making future plans with me? "I would love that." I can feel my cheeks heat as he places a hand on my thigh and backs out of the driveway.

———

"You made it!" Summer says when we walk in her house. "And you brought the hunky EMT. Or are you a firefighter?"

Hardy smiles, throwing an arm around my shoulder. The move feels claiming, and I sink into him. "Both, actually."

"He's not wearing a sweater," Raven says flatly, crossing her arms.

"But I have a dick in a box," Hardy says, shaking the box.

"Prove it," Raven challenges.

Hardy opens the box and proudly waves the vibrator for the girls to see. "Just so you know, it's not to scale."

"Wait, are you saying it's bigger or smaller?" Lucy asks, a sense of wonder in her tone.

Hardy's eyes cut to mine, avoiding the question.

"Oh my God. Good for you, Bella," Lucy gushes, and I look up at Hardy, trying to hide the blush on my face.

"I'm going to go grab us some drinks," Hardy says, kissing my forehead before he heads off to the kitchen.

"Oh, you two are *totally* banging," Summer says as the girls circle around me.

"Summer!" I scold, looking back at Hardy to make sure he didn't hear. "I can't deny it, and at this point, I'm not sure I want to."

"Called it! Pay up, ladies," Lucy says, sticking out a hand. Raven and Summer each slap a fiver into Lucy's palm.

"Ten dollars? That's all you bet?" I ask in shock.

"They said it was an inevitability," Raven says, pointing at Lucy and Summer.

"I knew when he came to the bar." Lucy smiles.

"I knew the minute I saw him walk into the PTO meeting," Summer adds.

"We weren't banging then," I say, but part of me knows they're not talking about when they first thought we were hooking up.

Hardy returns and hands me a red cup. I shift uncomfortably, not wanting him to catch on to our conversation.

He must sense my discomfort, and he peers down at me, searching my eyes for some kind of clue. "Is that mistletoe?" he says, his eyes lighting up as his fingers grip my chin and tilt my face up to his so he can seal his mouth to mine in a kiss. It starts sweet and chaste, but we lose ourselves in the moment as his hand slides up to hold my cheek, and I grip his waist while balancing my cup in the other.

"Okay, okay, we get it, get a room," Raven teases.

"I think it's sweet," Summer says.

I can hear Lucy laugh. "There's too much tongue in that to be considered sweet. And they're not even under the mistletoe."

Hardy pulls back, and I feel like one of those cartoon characters still pushing my lips out in a pucker looking for his.

"Fuck mistletoe. I don't need an excuse to kiss her," Hardy says to them, his eyes still locked on me. He leans in to kiss my cheek and then whispers against my ear, "I hope you know we aren't staying at this party for long."

"Your place or mine after?" I flash him a seductive smile.

"Given the layout of the bedrooms at my place and how loud I plan to make you moan, my place might be the safer option."

———

"I think the last time I got naked this fast was when Avery had a blowout while I was changing her and she sprayed me with poop," Hardy says, whipping off his shirt and kicking off his shoes at the same time.

"Totally what you want to hear when you're getting naked with your fella." I laugh, and he gives me a sheepish grin. "I'm just messing with you. Remember when you saw Isaac's massive poop? When you become a parent, your dignity goes out the window and you have to be able to pivot from poop talk to sexy time since you never know when the little semen demon is gonna cock-block you."

His shoulders shake in silent laughter. "I love how you make me laugh. You could've given me shit for ruining the mood, but instead you always lean into the humor, and I love that."

"You do, huh?" I say, standing in front of him in only my underwear as I take a step closer. He still has his pants on, and I thread my fingers through his belt loops and tug him against me.

"I do. I didn't think I'd ever find my sense of humor again, let alone joy. And I love that you've brought that back into my life. Into our lives."

That's an awful lot of loves. Is he testing the water to gauge my reaction?

"What else do you love about me? You know what a fan I am of lists."

"I love—"

"Daddy!" Avery's voice calls from the hall, and we look at each other in wide-eyed panic.

I grab my clothes and run to the bathroom, closing the door behind me. My breaths feel loud, but I try to stifle them as I quickly and quietly pull my clothes back on. I totally jinxed us with the mention of cock-blocking.

The room gets quiet, and I peek my head out and find it empty. I pull out my phone and send Lucy a quick text for a ride and locate my shoes, slipping them on as Hardy sneaks back in the room.

"Sorry, I need to go take care of this. Turns out she had a little too much water earlier and had an accident." He walks over to the closet and pulls out a set of sheets for Avery's bed.

"It's okay. Lucy's coming to get me. I realized you picked me up and then let Maggie go home so I needed a ride anyway."

"Fuck, I totally didn't think about all the logistics. I'm sorry." His brows are pinched, and he looks like this pains him, and I reach up to smooth the wrinkle between them.

"No need to apologize. I'll see you in the morning, hand-some," I say, stretching up on my tiptoes to kiss the tip of his nose.

I love the way he feels touching every inch of my skin, and even though the kiss is chaste, it makes me want him to throw me over his shoulder and manhandle me, but we can't seem to catch a break tonight.

"I'll make it up to you," he says, pressing his forehead against mine.

"I know you will. Now go take care of your little elf princess."

"Oh shit! I forgot about the elf!"

"Don't worry. I'll throw something together while you change her sheets and get her settled. I always have extra elf plans for school."

"I wish you could stay." There's a look in his eyes that makes me think he's wishing for more than just one night.

"Me too," I say, snuggling into his chest. "Text me in the morning." I bury my face between his pecs to hide the devious smile lighting up my face when I think about what I have planned for Sprinkle McPinkle Pants.

CHAPTER 23
HARDY

"**D**addy! Sprinkle McPinkle Pants made poops everywhere!" Avery yells as she runs in and jumps on my bed.

Rubbing the sleep out of my eyes, I look over and notice it's only six a.m. on a fucking Saturday. Why is my pride and joy waking me up at this ungodly hour on a weekend when I usually have to drag her out of bed at eight a.m. on a school day? I collapse back onto my pillow and close my eyes.

"Daddy, wake up. You need to see the poops!"

"I don't want to see elf poop. It's too early," I grumble as I roll over.

"But you have to come look, Daddy! And I heard him make the poops too."

I pop an eye open and am startled at how close her face is to mine. "What do you mean you heard it?"

"That's what woke me up! I heard giggles and then the poop splashes and when I went in the potty he was sitting on the seat."

"Wait, Sprinkle is a boy?"

"Daddy!" Avery scolds as she tugs me by the hand, pulling me out of the bed.

I reach over to the nightstand and grab my phone and notice a text from Bella.

> If you're reading this, it's probably morning and you forgot to charge your phone and you're just now seeing this text. Morning! I recorded a special sound effect as an alarm and hid my phone in the bathroom under the sink. There are several minutes of silence after, but you'll want to make sure to turn the alarm off, so it doesn't keep repeating. Isaac and I will be over later to pick you up

There's a dopey grin on my face as I read her text, and I start to reply and then realize that she won't see it since her phone is under Avery's sink.

When I get to the bathroom, I'm genuinely surprised by the scene she's created. It makes all the shit I've done with the elf look like amateur hour. Sprinkle is poised cross-legged on the seat of the toilet, his tiny elf ass propped slightly in the air as a Hershey's kiss sits underneath him. Several other kisses are inside the bowl and there are more unwrapped kisses on the floor. There's also glitter everywhere. On the back of the toilet, the seat, in the bowl, and on the floor.

"He could have at least made it into the bowl. Now I have to clean elf poop," I grumble as I squat by the sink and open the cupboard like I'm looking for cleaner. I grab the phone and turn off the alarm, tucking it back into place.

"I can help!" Avery says as she reaches down to pluck a piece of chocolate off the floor.

Since when does this kid offer to help? Maybe the elf isn't so bad after all.

She picks up the rest of the poops and throws them in the trash can. "I have to tell you something, Daddy," she says quietly once she's done.

"Okay?" I swallow nervously, worried she's going to tell me that she knows that the elf and Santa aren't real.

"Sprinkle left a bowl of poop candies in the kitchen too and I ate them all."

I sigh in relief. "Oh. Well, that's not the best breakfast, but I'm glad you were honest with me," I say, kissing her forehead as I stand.

"I wanted you to know. Miss Carlisle said it's okay to make mistakes, but we should admit them. And if Sprinkle tells Santa, I want him to know I did the right thing."

Something cracks in my chest at her admission. It's one of those moments of extreme pride and love that make your heart feel like it's going to burst out of your chest. They may not happen as often as we'd like, but when they do, they make all the shitty moments of parenting worth it. And this one is all because of Bella.

When Bella shows up with Isaac a few hours later, I'm overwhelmed with love when I see her. I want to tell her about my moment with Avery. I want to throw her against a wall and worship her body. But more than anything, I want to make sure she knows how grateful I am that she's in our life. That she helped me save Christmas. And that she brought me back to life. I never thought I would fall in love again after Lydie died, and while she can never be replaced, Bella has been the perfect addition to our world, bringing us exactly what we needed to heal and to love again.

"You couldn't have set the alarm for anything later than six?" I tease as she leans in to hug me once the kids run into the kitchen. I slip the phone into her hand.

"Oh shoot! I totally forgot to change that." She smiles sheepishly, and I can't tell if she's kidding or not.

"I'm going to punish you later for that," I say, swatting her ass as I follow her toward the kitchen.

"Oh, I'm counting on it," she says over her shoulder.

"Are we ready to go?" Isaac asks excitedly.

"Where are we going?" Avery asks, matching his energy.

"Well, Butterfly, today is the day that we do random acts of Christmas kindness."

"We call them RACKs," Bella says, doing a little shimmy with her chest that makes her tits jiggle.

"Mom, I told you to stop making that joke," Isaac groans.

"It's fine. Everyone appreciates a good RACK."

"I know I do," I say, raising my hand.

"You two are gross," he says, rolling his eyes.

"What's gross?" Avery asks.

"Nothing," the three of us say in unison.

We load up into my truck as Bella changes the radio to a station that plays only Christmas music. When I turn to look at her, she has the biggest smile on her face, and it nearly takes my breath away. She is so fucking beautiful, inside and out.

"What's the plan, Bells?"

She shakes her head at the mention of her nickname, making the bell on her Santa hat jingle. "Every year, we spend a day doing random acts of Christmas kindness. When Isaac was little, we would do one a day. As he got older, that wasn't always practical with our schedule, so we decided to make it one day."

"Yeah, but we still do other RACKs when we can randomly," Isaac pipes up from the back seat.

"What do these RACKs entail?" I ask.

She reaches into her bag and pulls out a stack of cards. "First, we're headed to the local nursing home to hand out Christmas cards and candy canes to the residents. I had my students make enough for each of the patients. The holidays can be lonely for a lot of them, and we want to make sure they get a visit from someone, a card, and a treat."

"Can I hand out the candy canes?" Avery asks.

"I got you, Butterfly," Isaac says, and I watch in the rearview mirror as he hands her several boxes of candy canes.

"This is a tradition we do every year, and I thought it might be fun for you to do with Avery in the future."

Something twists in my gut at her words, at her implication that this is something I would do alone with Avery next year. Everything we've done together this year has been special because of Bella and Isaac, and I want to continue these traditions with them next year and for many years to come.

I barely have time to dwell on that thought before she's giving me directions to the nursing home. We spend a couple hours passing out cards and candy and even play a few board games with the residents.

When we stop for lunch at a drive-thru, we pay for the people behind us, and just after we've finished our food and are driving to our next RACK, Isaac starts shouting.

"Trash cans! Mom, I see trash cans."

"I'm going to need you to flip a bi—" She looks in the back seat at Avery and corrects herself. "Make a U-ey. We've got trash cans."

I do as I'm told. "What am I missing? What's so special about trash cans?"

"This was one of Isaac's favorite RACKs when he was little. We would walk through the neighborhood on trash day and bring in people's cans. It was free and easy, and he was obsessed with the garbage truck back then."

I pull into the neighborhood and end up staying in the truck, creeping along as the three of them run up the street pulling in cans.

After every house is complete, Bella pulls out a few small bags of coins, and we head off in search of vending machines to tape them to with notes about paying for their drink.

We're sitting in the truck as Avery and Isaac run out to tape a few on the machines when I pick up one of the bags and look at the card printed in it. "Did you make these?"

"Yeah. It's a little weird to just tape a bag of money to a soda machine, so I print out little cards with fun sayings and explain what a RACK is and encourage people to pay it forward and post on social media."

The kids climb back in the car, and Isaac suggests we park so we can go shop for items to donate. Then we head into the store and grab items for a local food pantry, winter hats and gloves to donate, and a few toys to drop off.

I don't think I've ever had this much fun shopping before, and Avery doesn't even complain in the store once. At check-out, we end up paying for the people behind us and then pile back in my truck as Isaac directs us to a local church that has a mini food pantry outside of it.

He and Avery climb out and fill up the little cabinet and then we head over to a park with a little lending library. Isaac pulls a couple of books out of his bag and turns to Avery.

"Hey, Butterfly, did you know that Santa has a secret program?"

"No, he doesn't."

"It's true," he insists. "Anyone that donates their old toys or books gets extra checks by their name on the nice list, and that means he brings you extra presents."

"Is that true, Daddy?"

I nod my head in agreement. "It's true. It's one of Santa's rules. But it only counts if you do it to help others. If you do it just to get more gifts, Santa will know, and it won't count."

Her eyes light up, and she digs around in the seat pocket in front of her, squealing when she finds a book. She runs out of the truck after Isaac, and they put their books in the little lending library.

Bella turns to me. "That was quick thinking. See, you're not as terrible at the Santa stuff as you thought." When she winks at me, it goes straight to my heart, making it race in anticipation.

We make several more stops handing out gift cards, waving at people we see at stop lights, and spreading kindness and Christmas cheer.

Despite it being a long day full of activities, Avery doesn't complain once. In fact, each time we finish a RACK, she's asked what we can do next, even making suggestions like picking up trash, which is how we ended up at the school, collecting litter from the grounds.

Isaac and Avery run up ahead, and I laugh at the way he challenges her to a contest to see who can pick up more trash, then falls behind to let her get a head start.

Bella walks up next to me, her arm linked through mine, and rests her head on my bicep as we watch them.

"You and Isaac do this every year?"

"Yup. Like I said, we used to do one RACK a day as a countdown to Christmas, but Jake never wanted to help so it was up to me to make it happen. And we did for a while, but the divorce made it hard because I didn't get to see him every day. Eventually we decided to cram as many into a single day as we could."

I'm in awe of her tenacity. Most people would fold under the stress of what Bella's endured, but she's turned every obstacle meant to dull her blade into an opportunity to sharpen herself into the woman she is before me. A tiny little ball of Christmas joy and cheer.

"I wish I could see life and people the way you do, but I've seen so many shitty things in this world that it's hard to find the good. How do you do it? How do you believe in people when they let you down? How do you find the good?"

"How? I take one bite of the cookie at a time instead of cramming the whole thing in my mouth and ending up with a bellyache. One bite. One day at a time. Because I need to believe there's good in people. To believe in something bigger than me."

She pulls back, stopping me in my tracks, forcing me to hear her words.

"You're right that there's so much shit in this world, but I choose to believe that there's more good than bad. And that's what Santa represents. It's goodness and light, people coming together as a whole for a greater purpose, to spread joy and love at Christmas. It's this unspoken understanding that everyone adheres to—well, unless you're an asshole. If a kid mentions Santa in front of anyone, that person immediately plays along, no matter what the kid says. If the kid says they don't believe you, you try to convince them. If you talk about Santa as an adult, you always look around to check for little ears first. These are things we all do—no one teaches us this, we just do it. That's how I know people are good. Because their base instinct is to protect the magic of Santa. That's what I love about it. That's why I believe in Santa. I choose to see the good in everyone. Even grumpy firemen."

I grin down at her like a stupid, lovesick fool. "I think you were always supposed to be part of our lives."

"It definitely feels that way. And I'm not complaining." She looks up at me as she grabs my gloved hands in hers.

We stand there, eyes locked for several beats, and I decide that if I want to have more days like this with her, I need to make it clear how I feel, especially after her earlier suggestion that Avery and I do this alone next year. If only we didn't get interrupted last night, I was so close to telling her then.

I blow out a deep exhale and push down my nerves, push down the doubt, push down the guilt, and decide that it's now or never.

"Remember that day you told me how you looked up your students' names to come up with their elf name?" I ask as her brow knits in confusion. "Well, I looked up what your name meant too."

"You did?" She sounds surprised by my admission.

"I did, and it couldn't be more accurate. Your name means pure heart, and you, by far, have the purest heart of anyone I've ever met. You love with your whole heart, your whole mind, and your whole soul. I've never met another person like you, and I don't think I ever will."

"So, I shouldn't ruin this moment with a dick joke?"

I throw my head back in laughter. "Fuck, I love you."

My pulse quickens as the biggest smile lights up her face. "You love me?"

I slide my hand into her hair, pulling her close to me. "I really fucking do. I love your patience, your kindness, how much you care about everyone around you, even when they don't deserve it. I love the way you love my daughter. There's not a thing about you that I'm not wildly, madly, deeply in love with. And now I'm going to kiss you before you can make a dick joke."

Her laughter is cut short when I press my lips against hers, and then I'm wrapping my arms around her as I pull her body flush with mine. The kiss is slow and tender, erasing everything around us so that there's only us and this moment that feels bigger than both of us.

When we pull back, breathless and panting, I lean my forehead against hers.

"I can't help but notice you didn't mention Lefty and Righty in your little speech," she says, and I bark out a laugh. "Seriously, though, when I talked to you at that PTO meeting, you were so raw and vulnerable. I could tell how much Avery meant to you, and I think part of me fell in love with you at that moment. But you barely cracked a smile back then, and it became my mission to bring joy to both of your lives. Because I love you too, more than I could ever express with words."

And that's exactly what she's done. She's brought us joy. And laughter. And the magic of Santa. But more than all of that, she brought me back to life, and I will do everything in my power to show her how grateful I am.

CHAPTER 24
BELLA

"Are you ready for your next Santa lesson?"

I lead Hardy into the kitchen where my Aunt Delilah is pulling ingredients out of the fridge. He looks at the baking tools on the island. "What the hell is this?" he asks, holding up the penis cookie cutter.

"It's a penis. You're an EMT, shouldn't you know that?" I say with a wink.

The answering scowl on his face is priceless. "I know it's a penis. Jesus Christ."

"He is the reason for the season!" Aunt Delilah chimes in.

He shakes his head, growing more frustrated at our antics. "I thought you said we were making cookies. What do you need this for?" he asks, holding the cookie cutter by the tip, waving the balls around while he speaks.

How the fuck do I explain this? I'm madly in love with this man, he just told me he loves me, and I don't want him to regret that decision. And even though I'm slightly worried my brand of crazy will scare him off, I opt for honesty. If this relationship is going to last between us, he needs to know what he's in for with me. And my crazy sorta aunt.

"When I had a bachelorette party back in the day, my maid

of honor got penis-shaped everything, including that cookie cutter in your hand."

"I was her maid of honor." Delilah pokes her head out of the fridge.

"More like maid of dishonor." I laugh as she sets a carton of eggs on the counter.

She smiles back at me. "I wear the title proudly."

"The point?" he says, trying to rein us back in as his eyes shift toward the hallway, probably looking for Avery. But I'm undeterred since Isaac knows to distract her while we give him our cookie history.

"Honey, you have your big meaty paw wrapped around the point of that thing. Just look at the way you're gripping that shaft." Delilah cackles, and I lose it.

He drops the cookie cutter onto the counter, crossing his arms. "For fuck's sake."

Wiping the tears from my eyes, I continue, "Anyway, I tucked all the penis paraphernalia in a box in the basement so Isaac wouldn't find it."

Delilah shakes her head in agreement. "Poor thing didn't want to traumatize the boy."

"A few years ago, around Christmas, I sent Isaac down there to get my cookie cutters so we could make Christmas cookies. And since men seem to have such a hard time locating things that are clearly labeled…"

"And right in front of them," Delilah adds.

"Exactly. He couldn't find them. Despite the see-through bin clearly labeled 'cookie cutters,' my genius of a kid opens four boxes, all of them also clearly labeled with their contents, until he finds the gem of a cookie cutter you were just stroking."

He straightens. "I was not stroking it."

Delilah unwraps the butters, plopping them into the mixing bowl. "There was some stroking going on."

"Is she always like this?" he asks, gesturing a thumb at her.

"I am, and I'm a delight," she volleys back.

"That you are. You're getting after-school Delilah, not Principal Adams. Back to what I was saying. My kid comes running upstairs, proud of his discovery."

"He never did find the rest of the cookie cutters," Delilah says, throwing away the butter wrappers as she pulls out the sugar.

He watches in awe as Delilah and I work together as a team, her mixing as I grab the rest of the dry ingredients. "So, you made dick cookies?"

"I'm a single mom who survives off an IV drip of coffee. If it made him happy, I didn't give a fuck what shape it was. And he thought it was funny. It was one of the first times I'd seen him laugh since the divorce. So, we made dick cookies."

"But we didn't stop there!" Delilah adds.

He shakes his head "Why do I get the feeling I'm not going to like where this is headed?"

I smile at him across the island. "It became a tradition in our house. Anyone can have a cookie decorating contest, but only the elite make cock cookies."

Delilah comes up beside me, wiping her hands on her apron. "I wanted to call them dick cookies because it sounded softer."

"No one wants a soft dick in their mouth, Delilah." We break out into laughter, realizing what I just said. "Besides, I like the way cock cookies sounds. The alliteration. Cock cookies. It has more oomph than dick. Cock feels heftier in your mouth."

"I'd like a hefty cock in my mouth," Delilah says.

"Gives new meaning to eat a dick, eh?"

We dissolve into another fit of laughter. This is my happy place during the holidays, in my aunt's kitchen, surrounded by laughter, making phallic cookies. "Like I was saying, we have a cock cookie competition. Say that three times fast."

"Cock cookie competition. Cock cook—"

I laugh, cutting my aunt off. "I didn't mean to actually say it. "

"So, this cookie competition," Hardy prods, sounding interested.

"Say cock," Delilah interrupts.

His cheeks flush. "I'm not saying that."

Delilah gives him a curious look. "You a prude or something?"

I step up next to him, shooting her a look. "Leave the man alone." Then I turn to him to finish my story. "So, we have a competition. Some years we see who can make the most realistic cock."

"Do you think that's a good idea to do with your kid?" He sounds skeptical, and I would worry that he's questioning my parenting when I remember he's a girl dad.

"It was his idea!" Delilah laughs.

Placing an arm on his, I continue. "What you're forgetting is that I'm a boy mom. We're a different breed. Cocks and balls are an everyday occurrence for us. We don't scare easily. Remember how I drove around with a cock on my car not too long ago?"

Delilah laughs. "Ned told me about that."

"I saw Ned that day, and he didn't say anything to me!"

"Well, you know Ned," Delilah says, waving it off.

"Back to the competition. So, some years, it's all about realism. Another year we tried to see who could take their cock and disguise it into something completely different with just icing and decorations."

"I called it hide-a-willy!" Aunt Delilah exclaims.

"Last year, we took it a step up from that and allowed alterations to the dough, so you could cut up the cock or twist it into different shapes to disguise it.

"A puppetry of the penis but with cookies!"

He's not even phased by my aunt's interjections at this point.

"I'm not sure what we'll do this year, because it's not like you can just go to Pinterest for ideas for this sort of thing. But I'm sure we'll come up with something," I say as I scoop out the flour and place it on the island.

"We could do tattoos, or piercings. The ladies love those," Delilah suggests.

"I mean, that's cool and all, but we need something that really stands out. Something that pops."

"What about that picture you sent her the other day? The elephant trunk?" Hardy asks.

"Oh, thank you, I totally forgot I made that one. We could do an animal theme!"

"I knew the shape of that cookie looked off. Makes sense now," he says, shaking his head. "And the Only Fans joke. Only Cookies, because they're all penises, makes way more sense now."

Delilah looks at me. "Do you think we could make a legit OF account and get away with just posting cock cookies anonymously? There's someone who would pay to see that, right?"

"I dunno, seems risky. That sounds like an after-retirement side hustle," I say, tapping my chin.

"This is great and all, but I can't let Avery make cock cookies. She's six, we have not had the birds and the bees talk, and I'm not going to let a penis cookie cutter force my hand on that."

Isaac walks in right as I'm zooming in on the nuts-turned-elephant cookie. "Oh, that's a good one. Text it to me? I want to show my friend the nuts on that one."

"We're not showing our nuts to anyone," I say as he busts out laughing.

"You walked right into that one, Mom."

Hardy tilts his head in confusion.

"Isaac got tired of me always saying 'that's what she said,' so now he tries to set me up to say the most unhinged things."

A toothy grin lights up Isaac's face as he looks at Hardy while he opens the fridge. "She makes it way too easy."

Hardy scrubs his hands down his face. "Can we get back to the cookies? I'm not letting my daughter make cock cookies."

"Yeah, I was at least ten when we started," Isaac agrees, taking a bite of an apple.

"He's right," I say to Delilah.

"I guess we could go the traditional route this year." Delilah sighs reluctantly.

"Thank you," Hardy says as his shoulders relax.

I gather up the cock-ie cutters and pull out a bin with traditional Christmas-shaped ones.

"Giraffe!" Avery shouts.

"In the kitchen, Butterfly."

"There you are," she says as she runs in and pulls a chair up to the island to help. "Is it time to make cookies now?"

"We're almost done mixing the dough. Why don't you go ahead and pick out the cookie cutters that you think Santa will like best?" I lay out several options for her to choose from.

"We should use ones that won't burn," Avery says as Hardy rubs at the back of his neck.

"In that case, I'm going to rule out this candy cane one because it's not as thick and that could burn easily if we aren't paying attention," I say.

Avery nods thoughtfully as she taps her finger on her chin. "I want to do the tree, the sock, and the bomb," she declares proudly as she holds up the tree, stocking, and ornament cookie cutters.

"The bomb?" Hardy mouths to me, and I nod to let him know I got this.

"I think that's a great idea. I've never heard of a cookie bomb. What would it look like?"

"Like one of those black bombs in the old cartoons daddy likes."

Hardy and I share a knowing glance.

"Would it look like an actual bomb, or like a bomb-shaped ornament?" I ask, trying to gently push her in the ornament direction.

"Like a real bomb," she says as if that was the most obvious thing in the world.

"Got it. So does it explode like a real bomb?" I ask.

"We could fill it with sprinkles. And then they would fall out when Santa bites into it!" she exclaims.

That's actually a really cool idea, and I look at Delilah, silently asking her if we could make that.

Delilah nods as she carries the dough to the island. "I think we could accommodate that if we make three bomb cookies, stack them, and hollow out the middle one to hide the sprinkles. It would be a thick cookie, though, so I think we should only make one like that for Santa."

Avery beams with excitement as we spend the next hour rolling out dough and baking trees, socks, and bombs. Delilah packs up half of the dough, popping it in the freezer while Avery and Isaac carefully decorate our test cookies. I smile down at Avery as she puts the finishing touches on her cookie bomb, filling it with sprinkles, before smooshing the cookies together with a generous amount of icing.

"How does this look?" she says, proudly holding up the bomb.

Isaac leans over her shoulder and pretends to take a bite, chomping comically around her while she squeals and tries to protect her cookie. "Giraffe, no!"

Her squeals and giggles warm my heart, and I look over at Hardy. I swear there are tears in his eyes as he mouths "Thank you," and holds his hand over his heart.

"We have to save this one for Santa," Avery exclaims.

"Actually, you can eat that one, if it's okay with your dad. This was just a test run. We have extra dough in the freezer ready to make fresh cookies, so Santa doesn't have to eat ten-day-old ones."

Hardy nods, but it's in vain, because Avery is already shoving half the cookie in her mouth as sprinkles rain down her shirt.

"At least we know the cookie bomb works," Delilah says, pointing to the mess.

CHAPTER 25

BELLA

We're at the school to put the finishing touches on everything the night before the Workshop opens. Summer, Raven, and Lucy are helping while all our kids run around. They started out helpful, but it's quickly devolved into a game of tag, and we're all too tired to put a stop to it.

Hardy walks in carrying the Santa chair, and his face lights up as soon as he sees me.

"Oh, the hot firefighter is *totally* in love with you," Summer says.

"Called it! Pay up, ladies," Lucy says, sticking out a hand for Raven and Summer to each slap a dollar into her palm.

"Two dollars? Last time it was ten!" I say, trying not to laugh.

"After that night at the Ugly Sweater party, I think we all knew," Lucy says, pointing at Raven and Summer.

"That man is so gone for you," Summer says with a sigh.

Before Raven can add anything, Hardy walks over with the chair, and a silence falls over us. "Where do you want this?" he asks, never breaking eye contact with me.

"Now I see it," Raven says dryly as Summer and Lucy slap a hand to her stomach.

"We totally weren't talking about you," I say awkwardly as he sets down the chair.

He's next to me in two steps as he grabs my hand and pulls me into a relatively chaste kiss. I can hear the girls making catcalls behind me, but I'm totally wrapped up in this man.

When he pulls back, he leans in, his lips ghosting my ear. "That'll give you something to talk about." His voice is husky and full of promise.

Then he straightens up and addresses me normally. "So, where should I put Santa's throne?"

"You can put it over on the stage in front of the flats," I answer as I stare up at him in wonder and try not to think about how we defiled that throne. I'm so proud of him for being bold and also in shock that he made such a public declaration by kissing me since I know he's not a fan of the small-town gossip.

He lifts the chair and carries it across the room, but before I have time to digest his actions further, Isaac walks up carrying a box.

"What's in there?" I ask, and he shrugs.

I peel open the flaps and let out a little squeal.

"What is it?" Isaac asks as his curiosity gets the better of him.

"Don't tell Hardy, but I got him a Santa costume for tomorrow. And it comes with everything, even the sack!"

"Ooh, most of the sets I've seen don't include the sack," Summer says as she walks over, inspecting the box.

"How big is the sack?" Raven asks. "Is it an appropriate size? Can it hold all the gifts?"

"Does the sack match the rest of the outfit?" Lucy asks.

"You know, I think it does! The sack totally matches the hat, just like the carpet matches the drapes." The girls cackle behind me.

"Oh my God, how old are you guys? Can you please stop

saying 'sack?' People are staring," Isaac grumbles as he turns a deep shade of red.

"Says the kid who drew a dick on my car. You can dish it out, but you can't take it?"

"Whatever. I'm going to go help Hardy," Isaac says as he stomps off.

"Shit, is that our future?" Raven asks.

All their kids are ten and under. I'm the only one with a newly minted teenager. "Yup. Be prepared, ladies. They turn into moody little jerks."

"Lay off it, Chuck," Amber says, walking past us in a huff with her husband close on her heels. We do the obligatory back-away-and-look-around move, but we're all secretly hanging on every word of their exchange.

"Did he smell like booze to anyone else?" Lucy asks, holding her fingers under her nose.

"He smells like that at work all the time," Raven tells us. "I've said something to our supervisor, but they used to play football together in high school, so my complaints go unheard."

"There are kids around. He really shouldn't be doing that at a school." Summer crosses her arms.

"He shouldn't be doing that anywhere. And I don't disagree with anything you all are saying, but I need this to go smoothly tomorrow. We're going to keep our heads down and run interference if we need to, but I'm not saying anything to Amber. I don't need her to make my life any more miserable." And God forbid she tries to ruin what I have going with Hardy.

"Who cares what Anal Amber thinks?" Lucy huffs.

We all burst into laughter.

"Oh my God, that name is so going to stick!" I wheeze.

Raven looks between us, slightly confused. "Are we calling her anal because she's uptight or because—"

"Because she likes it *up* her *tight* hole?" I finish for her, and our fit of laughter continues.

"You have to stop. I'm going to pee my pants," Summer wheezes.

Hardy walks up to us and surveys the group. "Do I want to know?" he asks, turning to me. I shake my head. "I've got everything ready on the stage so you can do the Santa pictures. And Isaac is almost finished setting up all the tables. Then we can start laying out all the items. The prices are broken down by section with the cheapest near the door and the most expensive on the opposite end."

I've never wanted to mount someone more.

The girls try to stifle their laughter, and I look over, feeling my cheeks heat.

"I think that was an inside thought." Summer winks.

Hardy gives me a grin. "I think we can arrange that later." He plants a peck on my cheek. "I forgot to ask, who did you hire as Santa?"

If my cheeks were pink, they're red now. I avoid eye contact with him, looking at the girls, silently pleading for help.

"Bells." His voice is stern yet resigned, like he already knows his fate.

"He calls you Bells!" Lucy sighs.

"Aren't nicknames supposed to be shorter than your actual name?" Raven asks.

"Like jingle bells?" Summer raises an eyebrow.

"Actually, it's because I was wearing this hat while we—"

Hardy covers my mouth with his hand. "They don't need to know every detail," he chides as the girls whistle and fan themselves.

He removes his hand, and I turn to face him, grabbing his arms. "Don't be mad. I couldn't find anything in your size locally, so I had to order it, and I really hope it fits you." I walk my fingers up his chest slowly as I lower my voice. "Maybe you can try it on for me tonight."

"We're not banging in the same outfit I'm going to wear in front of the kids," he whispers back.

"Maybe not before you wear it for the kids, but definitely after." I wink, reveling in the way the tips of his ears turn red.

A throat clears behind us, and when I turn to look, I see Lucy pointing across the gym. Chuck is waving his arms wildly, stumbling around while Amber stares at him with her hands on her hips. They're too far away to make out any words, but it's obviously a heated argument.

"What do you think that's about?" Lucy asks, taking a step closer to me right as Amber whips her head in my direction and looks me straight in the eyes. Then she turns back to Chuck gesturing in my direction.

"I think it's about you," Raven says to me.

Right then, Chuck stumbles into one of the theatre flats and knocks it over. A hush falls over the gym.

"I'm going to escort him out of the building. Excuse me, ladies."

I watch as Hardy strides across the gym and helps Chuck up. Amber looks embarrassed and apologetic, and she rushes over to pick up the set piece as another mom helps her.

"I swear, if she's trying to sabotage you, she's reached a new low," Raven says, crossing her arms.

"Based on the way she's trying to fix what Chuck knocked over and the embarrassed look on her face, I'm going to guess this wasn't planned," I say, looking away from the scene.

"It's very noble of you to be so forgiving. I don't think I possess that level of fortitude." Raven places a hand on my shoulder.

"Honestly, I think she's just insecure, and for some reason, I've become her punching bag. I'm not saying I want to be best friends with her or anything, but I think she acts the way she does to make herself feel better."

"Hurt people *hurt* people," Lucy says.

I clap my hands. "Okay, we've got a few hours before I turn into a pumpkin, so let's start laying out merchandise."

It's incredible the way this group of moms comes together. I truly believe that we could solve most of the world's problems if moms were in charge.

Before I realize it, an hour has passed. I'm lost in thought when a pair of strong arms snakes around my waist as a warm, hard body presses against me, his pine, bergamot, and smoky scent filling me with peace. "How'd it go with Chuck?" I lean back against his chest, looking up at him.

"It was fine. I was tempted to drop him off at the drunk tank to sleep it off, but I just ended up taking him home since I couldn't get a rideshare to come pick him up."

"Yeah, Ned is usually in for the night by eight."

"This town only has one driver available?"

"Don't sound so shocked. Sometimes we have two. That was really nice of you to do that for him. I know you can't stand him."

He shrugs. "You're rubbing off on me."

I wiggle my butt against him. "Oh, I'll rub off on you."

He shakes his head. "I totally walked into that one."

"You sure did. Seriously, though, I have to thank you for everything. I couldn't have made this Workshop happen without you. I just wanted to prove that I wasn't the hot mess Amber thought I was, that I could do something without screwing it up." The words feel raw in my throat, and he turns me in his arms, cupping my cheeks.

"You didn't need me to make this Workshop special. You created something magical. I just helped enhance it." He swipes at a tear that spills over my lashes.

"I could say the same for you. I've watched you give your all to make Avery happy. There isn't anything you wouldn't do to give her the perfect Christmas. I sprinkled the ideas on you like glitter, but you're the one that made the magic happen for her."

"Between my carpentry talents and your creative genius, we make a pretty good team," he says as he leans down, kissing my forehead.

Snuggling into his embrace, it hits me that he's right. I couldn't have created what he did, and he wouldn't have known what to build without me. Maybe I don't have to be everything all the time. Maybe we could use our individual talents to help each other beyond the holiday season. Isn't that what everyone wants in a partner?

When we leave the gym an hour later, it's completely transformed into a magical North Pole headquarters. The painted flats are arranged on the stage to make it look like a real Santa's Workshop with shelves full of toys. The Santa throne Hardy and I defiled sits center stage, ready to have Santa Hardy record all the wishes of good little boys and girls. There are cute little North Pole signs placed throughout the tables, and there are blankets of fake snow placed around the space to make it look like a winter wonderland. All the gifts are neatly laid on the tables, and I smile, knowing that won't last long as I picture students running around, grabbing items and throwing them into their baskets for their loved ones.

"You ready?" Hardy asks from the door as I look over everything one more time.

"Almost." I run over to the stage and grab the box with his Santa costume. "We can't forget this. You'll need to arrive in costume tomorrow, so you should take it with you."

We lock up the gym, and when I crawl into bed that night, I have trouble falling asleep, feeling like I'm a kid on Christmas Eve waiting for Santa as I think about how excited the students are going to be tomorrow to see what we've created for them.

CHAPTER 26
BELLA

I take back what I said about Halloween. The last few days of school before winter break suck donkey balls. I don't wish this hellscape on anyone. Just like Halloween, the kids are sticky, hyped up on way too much candy, and there are still costumes because every day is a different dress-up day. I'm staring at way too many little elves and Santas as everyone runs around the room trying to burn off the sugar.

And because it's snowing outside, recess is indoors, except the recess monitor is out sick today—and everything is set up in the gym for the Workshop this afternoon and evening, making it off-limits—so the kids have recess in their classrooms, and I lost the only thirty minutes of quiet I have built into my day.

But I love my job. *I love my job.*

"Miss Carlisle, can I use the bathroom?" Avery asks.

I glance at the clock. "Can you hold it for twenty more minutes when we go as a class?"

She shakes her head as she wiggles in place. She's already doing the peepee dance. Fuck.

"Okay, take the hall pass and hurry back, okay?"

"I will!" she chirps as she rushes to grab the pass and bolts down the hall, leaving the door ajar.

I push up from my desk, dodging multiple elves as I walk over to close the door behind her, but before I can get there, an elf knocks over the tub of crayons and I silently curse to myself as I bend over to clean the mess.

I'm halfway through picking them up when the fire alarm goes off.

Who plans a fire drill this close to winter break? I guess it is ideal though, since kids won't miss any instructional time. "Grab your coats and line up," I shout over the chaos. We shouldn't be outside long, but the snow is really starting to come down and I don't need any student popsicles.

Grabbing the safety bag off the wall, I usher kids into the hallway, and they line up against the wall. I hope this doesn't take too long. I want to go down and check on the Workshop one more time before kids start visiting.

"Do you smell smoke?" Lucy asks quietly as she walks next to me.

"Wait, is this real?" I whisper, careful not to draw any student attention.

"Probably just some burnt pizza in the cafeteria setting off a smoke detector," she says, but looks uncertain. We push through the doors at the end of the hallway, the bitter cold hitting our faces as we usher the kids away from the building. Once we get to the parking lot, the kids line up, and I move down the row counting heads. We've done this twice already this year, so they know the drill by now.

"Twenty-two. Twenty-three. Everyone's here," I say right as a fire truck turns into the parking lot, pulling close to the opposite end of the school near the gym.

When I look over at Lucy, there's panic on her face. "Crap. This is real, and I'm short one." She pulls out her roll and calls out each kid by name, and when she gets to Melissa, a tiny little blonde second-grader darts out of my line and into hers.

"Wait, now I'm missing one." I pull out my roster when it hits me. "Avery!"

Panic claws at my chest as I walk up and down the line looking for her. I thought she came out with us. And there's a fire truck here, which means this could be a real fire and not a drill.

Isaac's class must be close by because he comes running up. "Did you say Avery? Where is she?" he asks, looking around.

"She went to the bathroom and then I was cleaning up crayons, and then the fire alarm went off. I forgot she was gone in all the confusion."

"Avery! Butterfly! Where are you?" Isaac calls out.

I can see several of his classmates pointing at us and laughing, but their demeanors change when several of us start panicking, shouting her name.

"Avery! Avery Williams!" I call out, looking around the other nearby groups. When I turn back to Isaac, he's gone. "Isaac?"

"Oh my God," Lucy says as she points at the building, and I see Isaac slip into the doors as a plume of black smoke rises from the back of the building.

"Isaac!" I yell, tearing after him, but he's too fast and the building is too far. When I get to the door, a firefighter blocks my path, holding up a hand to prevent me from entering.

"Mike?" I say, recognizing him under his gear as I pant, out of breath.

"Bella, sorry, I can't let you in the building."

"My son Isaac just ran inside," I say, trying to gulp in air. I'm going to hyperventilate.

"He must've run past when I was clearing a classroom. I'll call it in to the guys. What does he look like?"

"About my height, thin, floppy blond hair like an alpaca. He ran back in looking for Avery."

"Hardy's Avery?"

I nod as I try to get my breathing under control, but my heart is beating too fast and I can feel the rhythm in my ears. "She was in the bathroom and never came out. We couldn't find her outside."

"Shite." He talks into the radio on his shoulder, and either he's speaking in code or my head is getting lighter because I have trouble following what they're saying.

He places a hand on my shoulder. "My guy at the front door says he has eyes on Avery. She must've gotten lost in the shuffle and went out the front."

"Okay, okay, that's good," I say, bending over at the waist to grab my knees.

"Bella, are you okay?" His voice sounds distant and tinny.

"I'm going to need a medic over here. Female, early thirties, hyperventilating, possible panic attack, send a unit." I hear bits and pieces of what he says into his radio as I start to wobble.

Two hands grip my biceps, steadying me. I think they're Mike's. Seconds or minutes go by, I can't tell. The only word in my head and on my lips is "Isaac."

I faintly hear Mike giving me instructions to control my breathing, but I can't concentrate. My head feels so light and I'm having trouble holding it up when I feel him guide me to sit on the brick retaining wall.

"Bells? Baby, what's wrong?"

Is that Hardy? I can't open my eyes, and my entire scalp feels tingly.

"Hardy, I told you to stay back at the firehouse. I'm not letting ya in this building."

"I'm with the medical unit you called in," Hardy says. Is he angry? He sounds angry.

"You still shouldn't be here. We've got this."

"Isaac," I pant, still trying to get my breathing under control.

His warm arms wrap around me and I'm being lifted as he

places me onto a stretcher. "Bells, I need you to breathe. Can you take a breath and hold it for me? Breathe in through your nose for five seconds. One, two, three, four, five. And out through your mouth."

I follow his instructions, but I only last for three seconds before the breath comes rushing back out.

"I—I can't—Isaac."

"Where is he? Do you need me to get him?" he says, his voice laced with concern as I open my eyes and study his face. Does he not know? Did he not hear the call on the radio? Maybe they didn't say Isaac by name?

"In—In the building."

He blinks at me in confusion, and I see the moment it clicks for him. "Isaac's in the building?"

I nod, and suddenly my head feels woozy.

"Take it easy. Breathe."

"He went in for—for Avery."

"Avery's out front. She's safe. Delilah has her."

I nod as tears spill down my face. He grips my cheeks and swipes at my tears. It's so cold outside, I'm surprised his fingers aren't frozen to my face.

"I'm not supposed to be here for the fire call since it's Avery's school, but I was already headed this way when the call came in. Even though Avery's out and safe, they're not going to let me in the building. But I need you to understand that Isaac is safe, okay?

"You—you don't—don't know that." I gulp for air.

"You're right, I can't promise with one hundred percent certainty. But I can tell you that the fire is isolated to only the gym. I doubt Isaac went in there. And this is a great crew. They're going to find him."

There's chirping on his radio, and I catch the words. "Civilian located. Medical units are needed. Patient is unconscious. Meet on the east side of the building near the gym."

My breathing picks up, and we lock eyes. His head shakes

almost imperceptibly as if he's trying to convince himself that they're not talking about Isaac.

"Can you stand? I need to load this up so they can go to the gym. I can get another unit on the way for you."

"I'm fine," I rasp as he helps me off the stretcher and loads it into the back of the ambulance. He swings the doors shut and taps on the window, and it takes off to the other side of the building.

He walks back over to me, and I collapse into his arms. I should be embarrassed; my students are probably watching and I'm melting into his arms over here like a hot mess.

"Can—Can you hide me?"

He leans down like he's confused about what I'm asking. I'm not even sure I understand myself.

"I don't want my st–students to see—see me like this."

"Oh. I got you," he says, turning me so his body is shielding me as he rubs my arms like he's trying to keep me warm. "Now they just think you're cold, and I'm warming you up." His face is so full of love, and I want to revel in this moment, this public declaration, but I can't stop worrying about Isaac.

"They should've found him by now, right? Why haven't they found him?"

There's a commotion at the door and Mike walks out with Isaac behind him.

"Mom!" He runs over to me and throws his arms around me.

"Isaac! Oh, thank God. I was so worried about you." My face burns as hot tears spill down my frozen cheeks.

"I'm sorry, I had to find her. I looked in all the bathrooms before a firefighter told me she was safe and walked me out." His voice is wobbly, and I can hear the fear in it as he shakes in my arms. It could just be the cold, but I know it's not. He's grown to love Avery like she's his sister.

"I know you did, but you cannot run into a burning building. You scared the crap out of me."

"Your mom's right," Hardy says from behind me. "That was incredibly reckless and stupid." He pulls Isaac out of my arms and hugs him against his body, clapping a hand on his back. "So stupid and brave. And stupid. Thank you," he says, his voice breaking on the last couple words.

"Wait, if that call for a medic wasn't for Isaac, then who did they find?" I ask, turning toward Mike.

"I can't talk about an active investigation," Mike says as he walks back to the building.

Just as the panic subsides and I breathe a sigh of relief that all my people are safe, Mike's early words about the fire's location hit me. "Oh my God, the Workshop!"

CHAPTER 27
HARDY

The gym is a total loss. Half of the framework is burned, and the rest isn't structurally sound. You can see into the building from the outside that half of the Workshop is gone, and what's left is covered in snow and water from the hose.

"All that work. We worked so hard on this, and now it's gone. And there's nowhere for the kids to shop." Bella's voice breaks as she snuggles into my chest. We're huddled in the parking lot as the crew puts out the last embers. The students have long since gone home, and only a few of us are gathered.

"But everyone's safe," I say. "The kids are with Delilah, and no students were harmed."

"Oh my God, Amber was right. She knew I would screw this up, and here we are, one day left before break with nothing to show for it. I do ruin everything I touch. And I managed to ruin everyone's Christmas in the process."

I grab her shoulders and force her to look me in the eyes. "This is not your fault. You didn't ruin anything. You made magic, and something happened that was out of your control."

She grips my forearms, running her hands up and down. "I know that in my head, but my heart's a different story. I didn't start the fire, but bad things seem to follow me. My mom's accident wasn't my fault, my marriage ending wasn't my fault, but bad things keep happening, like the universe thinks I don't deserve happiness. How is this any different?"

I don't even know how to respond to that even though I know it's not true. But after everything she's done for me, for Avery, and for her students, I can't let her think that any of her thoughts hold merit.

"Sometimes bad things happen to the people that least deserve it. But you're so much stronger than the bad shit that happens to you. I've seen how you used that pain to sharpen your sword and defeat your adversaries. You have this incredible way of turning tragedy into hope, using your grief to make things better for others. You've experienced profound loss, yet you're determined to learn from it and make the world a better place because of it."

"So even if someone screws up Christmas, I can help them make it better?"

"Exactly."

"That's a fun way to describe my optimism." She chuckles. "Like I'm a badass spreading joy whether you like it or not. Like some little elf running around throwing glitter in your face saying, 'You're going to make this a Merry Christmas or else!'"

"Exactly. We'll get through this too. We'll figure something out for the kids."

She snuggles into my chest again just as something occurs to me. "What if it was Amber? She's had it out for you since you signed up. Do you think she would go this far?" I ask.

Her head pops up. "I don't know. She doesn't like me, but it seems more like her projecting her insecurities than actual hatred. I don't think she'd do this."

"Well, we'll find out once they wrap the investigation," I say as I pull her back against my chest.

"Bella!" a voice calls out, and I see Lucy run up, Summer and Raven close behind her. "Did you hear?"

"Hear what?" Bella asks.

"They made an arrest, or they will as soon as he's out of the ICU. It was Chuck. Apparently, he got so blitzed when Amber didn't come home last night that he came up to the school today looking for her and snuck into the gym. Rumor has it, he passed out on Santa's throne with a lit cigarette in his mouth."

"And everything around the throne was wood…and flammable," I say.

"Exactly," Lucy says.

"Why didn't Amber go home? We saw them fighting last night, but I don't know what it was about," Raven asks.

All four women turn to me.

"Don't look at me. He didn't say anything other than drunk ramblings when I drove him home."

"What are we going to do? Not only was this supposed to give our students an opportunity to shop for their families, but the proceeds were supposed to help the community. Tomorrow's the last day before break. We can't rebuild all this by then." Bella's shoulders slump, and I wrap my arms around her.

"We'll think of something," I assure her.

"Actually, that's why we're here," Summer says. "I talked to Ned down at the Chestnut Mountain Market, and he's agreed to let the students shop in his store this weekend. He said someone paid for his meal in the drive-thru recently, and he wanted to pay it forward."

Raven nods in agreement. "Several of the stores on Main Street are going to participate. Sandy at Chestnut Roasters said she wanted to help because someone paid for her soda on a vending machine. The hardware store, Chestnuts and Bolts, is in, and Meredith at Bookish Wonderland wants to help because she said a certain elf paid for her groceries recently. And Susy over at Peak Sweets was going on about kids bringing in the trashcans in her neighborhood. The whole community is helping. Everyone was inspired by your idea to collect donations and give back."

"We're going to hand out these special shopper cards that we designed," Lucy tells us. "I just need to print them at school tomorrow, and we can explain the process to the kids and send an email out to parents."

"There won't be wrapping, and it won't be a one-stop shop —" Summer starts.

"Actually, some of the stores are offering wrapping," Raven interrupts.

Bella perks up in my arms. "So, Christmas isn't ruined?"

I cup her face in my hands. "It's not ruined. And everyone is coming together for the community because of what you did."

"It's the magic of Christmas!" Summer exclaims.

CHAPTER 28
BELLA

The students were able to attend the last day of school—luckily the fire was isolated to the gym, and since it's mostly separate from the rest of the building, classes went on like normal. Well, as normal as the last day before winter break can be with kids who are hopped up on sugar and have no gym to run around in to burn off their energy.

Lucy was able to distribute all the Santa shopping cards so the kids can do their holiday shopping over the weekend. It's not going to have the same magical experience we created in the gym, but it'll be close. It's incredible the way the town stepped up.

Once the last of the kids leaves my room, I gather up my bag, pulling on my hat and coat. The binder I made for the workshop catches my eye on the corner of my desk, and I run my fingers over it, thinking about all the joy and agony it brought me. Okay, mostly joy with a little heartache at the end. But it also brought me Hardy, and I wouldn't trade that for anything in the world.

The door to my room swings open just as I finish packing up my bag. "Finally, Isaac. Are you ready to—" I look up and am surprised to find it's not my son standing there.

Amber shuffles her feet, looking down at the floor. "I owe you an apology," she mumbles as she picks at her nails.

"For what?" I ask, walking over to her as she leans against the doorframe.

"For ruining Santa's Workshop for you," she says softly.

Inside my head I'm screaming, *"I knew it, I knew you sabotaged me!"* but when I examine her face, she swipes at her nose and then rubs along her forehead like she's trying to shield her eyes from me. I instantly recognize the guilt, and I know that she had nothing to do with this. Just like I had nothing to do with my mom's accident, yet I still blamed myself, just like she's doing now.

"You can thank Chuck for getting drunk and passing out with a lit cigarette. The fire wasn't your fault."

"It kinda feels like it was."

She doesn't offer more, so I stare at her expectantly.

"I asked him for a divorce. The night we were setting up Santa's Workshop."

"Is that what you two were fighting about?"

She nods as she shifts, visibly nervous. "Look, I don't have my life all figured out like you."

I stifle the laugh building inside of me. For once it seems like she's being genuine and not poking at me.

"You have all these friends, and your kid likes you. And now you have this great guy who seems to really care for you, and I was jealous. I know it may seem like I have this amazing life, but it's all for show. It's a house of cards that is a light breeze away from collapsing. The truth is that things in our marriage have been awful for a while even before Chuck got drunk that night and talked about your past. And I know what he said wasn't your fault, but I was embarrassed, and I took it out on you. I kept thinking that if everyone kept talking about you, no one would notice the disaster our marriage was."

"That's really shitty of you, Amber," I say, crossing my arms.

"I know and I'm sorry." Her face is so sincere as her brows knit, and she clasps her hands in front of her.

"I forgive you. I know it's not easy to admit all this."

"And then you and Jake divorced, and I felt even worse, but again the focus wasn't on me and my crappy marriage."

"No, it was on mine." I let out a sardonic laugh. "But Jake and I didn't end our marriage because of all the stuff Chuck said at the bar that night. It was a long time coming. You shouldn't blame yourself for that either."

"He drinks a lot, ya know. And I told him that I was done."

"Good for you. You deserve better than that. No one deserves to be around that."

"Right. Well, he didn't like that. Once Hardy dropped him at home, he drank more. And when I didn't come home, he stayed up drinking all night and ended up in Santa's Workshop when he came looking for us at school the next morning."

"You are not responsible for his actions," I say, looking into her eyes. "And it takes guts to admit all of this to me. It's brave, and you should be proud of that."

"It doesn't feel brave. I feel like a hot mess. I feel like everyone's talking about me and what a total shit show I am."

"You wanna know a secret? We're all shit shows. Some days we're a massive dump, and then other days we're all backed up and it just looks like we've got it together. And some days smell worse than others. But at the end of the day, everyone poops. And we can point out the size, shape, and color of each other's turds, but we all make turds." I smile to myself, kinda proud of my profound poop analogy.

"Okay, why does that make so much sense?" she says, laughing.

"Because everyone poops." I wiggle an eyebrow at her, and she smiles.

"You're really weird."

"Thanks?"

"But I like you."

Before we can braid each other's hair around the proverbial campfire, Isaac walks up behind her and clears his throat.

"I'm coming," I jokingly grumble before turning back to Amber. "Are you going to be okay? Do you need a place to stay? You're always welcome at our place."

"We're good, actually. We're staying at my mom's, but that's really sweet, especially after I've been so awful to you."

"We still have six days till Christmas. It's never too late to make it onto the nice list."

CHAPTER 29
HARDY

"Daddy! Daddy, wake up! It's Christmas!" Avery shouts as she climbs on the bed, jumping up and down, before crawling between me and Bella.

Since Avery decided she wanted Giraffe and Bella to celebrate Christmas with us, they spent the night. They've actually been staying over every night since Christmas break started. We were able to clear some space in the finished part of the basement for Isaac to set up an air mattress so he could have his own area too.

"Coffee," Bella grumbles sleepily, curling up tighter. I roll out of bed, pull on some sweats, and head downstairs with Avery.

Isaac is sitting at the kitchen table when we walk in. "I already started the coffee for Mom. Hey, Butterfly, did you see what Santa did? Go look."

She runs over to the front room with the tree and is stopped by a giant wall of paper blocking off the room.

"He did it!" Avery squeals as she jumps up and down.

"What's happening now?" I ask, looking very perplexed at the wall of wrapping paper I definitely didn't put there. When I look over at Isaac, he just winks.

"I asked Sprinkle to wrap up the whole room. Bella said you have to ask Santa, but I forgot, and then Isaac said I could ask Sprinkle on Christmas Eve. And he did it!" she says, bouncing up and down.

Bella stumbles downstairs in a pair of flannel pajama pants and one of my old fire station T-shirts, her hair thrown up in a messy bun on the top of her head. She's never looked more beautiful, and I can't help but stare as she walks over and reaches into the cupboard behind me for a mug.

"Why are you staring at me like that? Do I have something on my face?" she asks through a yawn.

I set down my mug and pull her into my arms. "You look beautiful, and I can't take my eyes off of you." She shoots me a "yeah, right" look, and I hook my fingers under her chin, tilting her face to mine. "You are the embodiment of Christmas morning." I lean close to her ear. "Yawning cause you've been up all night wrapping gifts, disheveled, and in my T-shirt looking like you're mine, flushed because of how hard I fucked you last night, and totally and utterly beautiful. This is a sight I want to wake up to every day."

She pulls back and searches my eyes like she's worried I'm kidding. "You can't say things like that to me. I'll never leave," she says as she leans in to kiss me, and I pull back and hold her face. "Okay, I was kidding. Kind of."

"What if I wasn't?"

"Wait, what are you saying?"

"I know this probably seems fast, but I feel like I've known you for years, not two months. But I don't want to spend any more time apart. This week has been perfect, and I want to wake up to you every morning. You don't have to say anything, and we can figure out logistics later but—"

"Yes! I want to wake up to your grumpy face every morning too."

I pull her in for a kiss, keeping it short and sweet, but my heart feels so full of love for this little family we've made.

We eat breakfast quickly, just bacon and eggs, and Avery scarfs hers down, ready to break through the wrapping wall.

"Go brush your teeth."

Avery whines but reluctantly ascends the stairs as I join Bella and Isaac at the table after washing the frying pan.

"You know you're going to have to do that every year, right?" Bella says to Isaac.

"I know. But did you see her face?"

Bella smiles as she sips her coffee. "It's a pain in the ass to put up, isn't it?"

He laughs. "It is. But it was my favorite part of Christmas morning. Thank you for making it special for me."

"It wasn't me, it was Santa," she says just as Avery runs back in the room ready to boss us all around.

Her run through the paper wall was epic. Bella was able to sneak into the room and capture the whole thing in slow motion, and the look on my little girl's face when she saw the tree and stockings is one that will be imprinted on my soul forever.

Now, she's handing everyone their stocking, but the three of us watch her empty and open hers before we touch our own. Each squeal lights up my heart. She was excited last year, but it was nothing like this, and I worried that I wasn't capable of bringing this kind of magic back into her life.

"Hardy! Did you buy stocking stuffers right under my nose without me knowing?" Bella says, pulling me out of my thoughts.

"I did."

Her nose crinkles in the adorable way it does when she's trying not to cry, and I scoot closer to her on the couch, pulling her into me so I can kiss the side of her head as she continues opening her stocking.

"Blind bags! Did you get these when we went to Denver? Seriously, this is some next-level stuff. I am so impressed. How did you do it without me knowing?"

"Let's just say that kiss was a great distraction. And if Amber hadn't walked up, I would've grabbed a few more."

"What's so special about those anyway?" Isaac says, plopping onto the other side of the couch as he crams a cinnamon roll in his mouth. I swear this kid is always eating, but I guess I was too at that age.

"It's the gift you get to open twice!" she squeals, tearing open the bag and marveling over the contents.

"Daddy, look! There are new ornaments on the tree!" Avery says, pointing to a new princess ornament covered in entirely too much glitter for my liking.

I walk over to examine it, and sure enough, I don't recognize it. When I look over at Bella, she winks. It's amazing the way she and Isaac have seamlessly folded into our lives, combining their traditions with our own.

Avery is playing a game that Isaac coded from scratch just for her on an iPad he said his dad gave him that he didn't need anymore. The gesture is so touching and thoughtful.

The room is a mess, there's wrapping paper and ribbon everywhere, but there's one more present tucked into the corner of the room, and I drag it over to Bella.

"Hardy, this is huge!" Bella squeals.

"That's what she said," Isaac says, and then slaps a hand over his mouth. I look over, but Avery is too engrossed in her game to notice. "Sorry, force of habit. Mom makes it way too easy."

I chuckle at his astute observation. "I've noticed."

"Hey, I'm not that bad," Bella says.

"Open it," I say, gesturing to the giant box in front of her.

Everyone else has opened all their gifts, but Bella had insisted that she would go last. She eyes the box up and down, trying to determine the best course of action. "I'm pretty proud of the wrap—" Before I can finish complimenting my own wrapping skills, Bella tears into the box as little scraps of paper fly all around her. It's almost comical the way her arms are flailing as she continues ripping, but I see the minute she reveals enough of what's underneath.

"Oh my God, Hardy. Is this—is this a giant *Die Hard* inflatable of Nakatomi Plaza exploding?"

There's a stupid grin on my face as she scrambles to get up, nearly slipping on a large piece of wrapping paper as she runs over and throws herself into my arms.

"Does this mean we aren't going discount inflatable shopping tomorrow?"

"We can still go, but I wanted you to have something to add to your Christmas collection."

"So, you admit that *Die Hard* is a Christmas movie?"

I nod my head. "*Die Hard* is a Christmas movie."

She presses her lips against my ear, squeezing me into a tight hug. "I don't think I've ever heard you utter sexier words."

Leaning back, I kiss her nose and then nod toward Isaac. "There's one more thing. Isaac made you something."

She climbs off my lap and walks over to Isaac as he hands her his phone. "What am I looking at?"

"Hey, Avery, you should go put your princess dress on and show Bella," I suggest. "I bet it will look great next to the sparkly palace."

"That's a great idea," she says, taking off for the stairs.

Bella's brow pinches. "I've seen that dress before."

"I know. I just needed her to be preoccupied for a minute."

Isaac points to an app on his phone. "Tap the app with Santa on it."

She follows his instructions, and it's obvious she hasn't figured out yet what she's holding.

"This is cool. Are these like little Santa games? Did you build this for Avery?"

"Kinda?" Isaac says.

"Keep exploring," I say.

"So kids play the games and earn nice points? And they can do chores and read stories to earn points too?"

"Yup. Now, hit the icon in the top corner of the screen."

She frowns. "It's asking for a password."

"Type 1234," Isaac says.

"You guys, what is this?" She swipes excitedly through the different screens. "Is this what I think it is?"

Isaac looks at me, his grin as big as mine.

"Did you build me an app for The Santa Rules?"

"Isaac did," I say, full of pride for the kid.

"It was your idea," Isaac says.

"This is so cool. Can I customize my tier to include anything I want?"

"You can," Isaac says, grabbing the phone and walking her through the other parts of the app. He's so excited to show it off, talking animatedly about it, and I can't help but tear up a little. "And there are message boards to connect with other parents, share recipes, and find volunteer opportunities."

She turns to me. "This has everything we talked about that night in the bar. And more. You listened to everything we said, and you made it real."

"It's the magic of Santa, and you've been a good girl—"

"Gross, guys."

"Wasn't being dirty that time." I laugh and then continue. "You are so good to others, and you deserve some of that goodness to come back to you. And this is a great way to share your idea and spread the magic of Santa with everyone."

"Thank you," Bella says, pulling me and Isaac into a three-person hug.

"This is the best Christmas ever!" Avery squeals as she runs over to us in her princess dress.

Bella is beaming ear to ear as I scoop Avery in my arms, and she gives me a big hug.

"And I got everything I asked Santa for."

"You asked him for the princess palace, I take it?"

She nods enthusiastically. "But I also asked him for another gift. A secret one."

"What was that?" Bella asks, coming up beside us. She leans into my side and I wrap an arm around her waist.

"I asked Santa for a family. And we're like a family. We do stuff together, like Christmas."

Oh, my fucking heart. I love this little girl so much. And the life we've created. And the family the four of us have forged.

EPILOGUE
BELLA

"Is it supposed to be this bumpy?" I ask nervously as we reach our cruising altitude.

"I can't believe you've never been on a plane before," Hardy says as he squeezes my hand over Avery's seat.

"I've been on a plane before, but not many. And none this bumpy." I clamp down on his hand. I'm trying to sound brave so I don't scare Avery, but I'm failing miserably, and I'm worried I won't make the two-and-a-half-hour flight without shedding some tears.

My fear of flying was always a point of contention with my ex, and we would only take trips that were within driving distance. Or he and Isaac would travel without me. But I'm determined to overcome this and try new things with Hardy.

Isaac threads his hand between the window and the seat in front of me, and I grab it with my other hand, thankful for both of my guys.

"It's only bumpy over the mountains, then it gets better," Avery says, leaning against my arm.

"Great, even the six-year-old is braver than me," I say with a self-deprecating laugh.

"I think you're incredibly brave," Hardy says. "I know how

hard this must be for you, but you're doing it anyway. That's brave."

Huffing out a breath, I silently agree and focus on my breathing. I'm not sure what's got my nerves so twisted, but it likely goes back to my accident with my mom. I get nervous when driving in the snow, and apparently nervous in the sky.

Once we clear the mountains, the ride does get smoother, and just as I'm getting relaxed and comfortable, we start our descent into Los Angeles.

Hardy planned a trip to California for us while we're on summer break. I'm pretty sure it was Avery who begged to go to Disneyland until he finally relented. It's our first trip out of the state together as a family, and I couldn't be more excited. Well, except for the flying part.

When we land, and I kiss the ground for a solid five minutes—figuratively, of course, because ew, gross—we take a rental car and head out to explore the city.

I'm stunned when Hardy pulls into the Beverly Hills Hilton. "Umm, Hardy, this looks fancy."

He puts the car in park and leans over to kiss my temple. "It's okay. I got a great deal." He tosses the keys to the valet, and a man hurries over to help us with our bags.

Check-in is surprisingly quick, and Avery doesn't whine at all. It helps that Isaac keeps her entertained.

When we get to the room, he hands Isaac a key and then points one door down.

"Did you get adjoining rooms?"

"I did," he says against my ear before kissing my cheek.

The rooms are nice, and the kids are excited to have their own beds, and I laugh as Avery runs between the rooms, bouncing on all the beds, determined to find the best one.

I grab Hardy's hand and pull him against me. "Thank you for planning all of this."

"Haven't you figured out yet that there's nothing I won't do for the three of you?" he says as he leans down and kisses my forehead. I want to push him backward onto the bed and have my way with him, but I refrain.

"Are we ready to go?" Isaac asks, uncharacteristically chipper.

"I wanna go too!" Avery whines.

"We're all going," Hardy says, corralling us toward the door.

"Where are we going?" I ask.

"You'll see," Isaac says over his shoulder.

I look back at Hardy, and he shrugs as he tugs on his neck. That's his nervous tic. But why is he nervous?

Once we're on the street, I squint in the California sunshine and slip my sunglasses on as Avery tugs on my hand, guiding me to follow her.

"How far is it, Daddy?"

"Not too far, but I can give you a piggyback ride if you want to save your energy," Hardy offers as he squats in front of her, allowing her to climb on his back.

Do I shamelessly check out his ass? Yes. Yes, I do.

"I can feel your eyes on me, Bells." Hardy smirks over his shoulder as he extends his hand back for me to grab. And just like Thor's stupid hammer, my hand reaches for his, and he threads our fingers together.

The entire walk feels normal yet strange. Isaac is animatedly pointing out things along the way, and it's starting to feel like a diversion. I keep looking up at Hardy, but his brows are furrowed, and I can't tell if he's just squinting from the sun, or if he's stressed out about something. I know he's not a huge fan of crowds, so I chalk it up to that as I try to enjoy our stroll.

When I look up, there's a large cylindrical building in front of us, but I can see a familiar-looking building peeking out behind it. We walk a little further, and I gasp when I realize what it is.

"Oh my God, Hardy! Does that building look like Nakatomi Plaza, or am I imagining things?"

"You're not imagining things. It's Fox Plaza. It's where they filmed the exterior shots for *Die Hard*."

I cannot contain the squeal that comes out as I let go of his hand and run ahead, excited to see it up close. When I get to the steps, I peer up at it, doing a little shimmy, unable to hold in my excitement.

"Bella." Hardy's voice pulls me out of my stupor, and when he grabs my hand, I turn to see him kneeling on the ground with a ring in his hand.

My hands fly up to my face as my jaw drops open in shock. "I knew something was up."

"You did?"

I laugh nervously as a tear rolls down my cheek. "Isaac was way too excited to point out random buildings, and you looked anxious the entire walk over here."

"I just wanted to make sure everything went smoothly," he says, taking my hand. "Bella Carlisle, you are the love of my life, and I will forever be grateful that I answered that 911 call last October. You bring so much joy and magic to our lives. You're an incredible mother, an amazing partner, and the most caring person I have ever met. I would be lucky to be able to call you my wife, and if you'll do me the honor, I will spend the rest of my life loving you the way you deserve and making you proud to call me your husband. Will you marry me?"

"Say yes!" Avery squeals as she jumps up and down.

"Yes. Yes, I'll marry you," I rasp through tears, and before I can finish my sentence, Hardy shoots up, pulling me into him as he seals his lips over mine.

I can hear Avery's giggles and cheers, and Isaac's "gross," but I'm lost to this man and this moment.

When he pulls back, I grab his cheeks. "I love you too."

He gives me a quick peck and then slides the beautiful ring onto my finger.

"Wait, are we still going to Disneyland, or was this all a ruse?"

"We're still going," he says as he pulls me against him. "But we have to share a room with the kids at that hotel, so we better make use of our separate one tonight," he whispers against my ear.

"Are we ready for ice cream?" Isaac asks. "There's a place I saw on the way here."

"I want ice cream!" Avery says excitedly, and we make our way back toward the hotel.

"Want a ride, Butterfly?" Isaac asks, squatting down for Avery.

"Okay!" she agrees as she climbs onto his back.

My heart feels so full as we walk to get ice cream and start this new chapter as a family. And while we may not have another decade of Santa, I know we will have many more holiday traditions to come.

The End.
Want to find out what happens when Bella finally convinces
Hardy to wear the Santa suit?
Download the bonus scene at
https://BookHip.com/MKZPVJB

STAY IN TOUCH

I hope you enjoyed this holiday treat and would consider writing a short review and posting it on Amazon, Goodreads, Bookbub, or anywhere else you share book love.

Even a single sentence review helps other readers decide to take the chance on a new-to-them author. It can make all the difference for indie authors like me.

Want to know when I have a new release or get exclusive access to my works in progress? Let's keep in touch!

Follow me on Goodreads:
https://www.goodreads.com/author/show/55362142.Mya_More

Follow me on Amazon:
amazon.com/author/myamore

Join my reader group:
https://www.facebook.com/share/g/1ZnWm8uSUT/

ACKNOWLEDGMENTS

I cannot begin to tell you how many parts of my kids, my family, and our traditions helped shape this story. I literally can't tell you, because they would kill me if I shared which ones are real and which ones are made up. Though if you follow me in IG, you can probably figure out some of the ones that are inspired by real life.

I asked my eldest child to give me a name for a cool teenage coder character. He picked Isaac and immediately demanded I thank him in my book. Like I told my youngest, I was not about to put his name in a smut book so I was told to refer to him as my eldest because it sounded fancier than oldest. Thanks, Dingdong. They also agreed to create the cover pose for me so I'd have something to send my cover designer. And I will cherish that picture as future blackmail when Prom rolls around.

This book was supposed to be a standalone but my wonderful editor Sarah told me I need to make it a series so look out for future books with the moms! And thank you Sarah for the tight deadlines you made work for this! I wish you all the Hozier and Sleep Token concert tickets. I cannot tell you how much I appreciate you answering all my late night questions and ramblings.

Amanda, thank you for being the sweet cheerleader for my books! Amanda, Bianca, and Layla, by the time you read this you better be packing for Philly. I can't wait for us to live narrate the rest of Ethan's book for Layla. Thank you ladies for being my support system. I love you all!

Thank you to all of my lovely beta readers! Amanda, Angelica, Ashley, Hannah, Stacey, Jazmine, and Rachel. Your feedback was so valuable in refining this story. I appreciate each and every one of you.

Being an indie author can feel isolating at times, but I am so thankful for this community of women who have helped me along the way. Berlin, LJ, Erin, Mauve, Sky, Taccara, Loren, Ruby, Jen, and Kay. From Sleep Token clips, way too many voice memos, TMI stories (there's no such thing!), multiple timezones, not entirely enough thirst traps, supportive husbands, sprints, blurb dodging, creamy peens, raccoons and possums, and all the laughs. You ladies have lifted me up, supported one another, and offered comfort and advice and I appreciate all of you. Let's conquer this romance world, one good pegging at a time!

To my Aries bestie Jen, I made this one shorter just for you. Now I'll know if you skipped this shoutout, you goof. I'm so glad our boys sat next to each other on the bus that day and became besties because you're stuck with me now. Love you!

Heather, I look forward to our phone calls and yearly visits. The next time meat pie asks you to pick up batteries, I'm tagging along! I hope he enjoys this book too and I promise the ninja death star will appear in one of these.

Thank you to all my Amores! I love my little street team! Thank you for loving my books and sharing them with others.

Your support means so much and I couldn't do it without you all!

Chris, you app building genius you. Thank you for putting up with my technical incompetence. I bow down to your genius. You are a coding mastermind and I'm grateful you married my best friend. THANK YOU!

Hey Coach, I love you. Thank you for your unending support. For tagging along at book events, buying us cookies, and donning scary book boyfriend masks. You are my ultimate HEA and I love you, grumpy bear. I will always want to yippee ki yay you, mother fucker.

ALSO BY MYA MORE

The Broken Series

All Her Broken Pieces

Bridget and Ethan's story. An age gap (she's older), forced proximity, black cat/golden retriever spicy romance.

All Our Broken Vows

Becka, Robert, and Bennett's story. An MMF, bi-awakening romance with found family, a single dad, and friends that become so much more.

All His Broken Rules

Emma and (John) Professor A-hole's story. An age gap, forbidden romance with a professor/student who break all the rules.

All Their Broken Promises

Coming 2026

The Chestnut Mountain Series

The Santa Rules

A holiday rom com with a single mom, a single dad, two kids, and a whole lot of fun.

The Lucky List

A rom com with a tired single mom, 2 active little boys, an Irish firefighter, and a whole lot of luck.

The Summer Plans

A rom com about a single mom with 3 kids, a single dad firefighter, an unforgettable vacation, and a second chance to get it right.

Coming May 21st, 2026

ABOUT THE AUTHOR

Mya has always had a passion for storytelling and has a background in theatre, film, and education. She lives in the Midwest with her husband and children, working a nonromantic job by day while writing romance at night. Her books are contemporary romance with more love, more spice, and more HEAs. When she's not writing, she enjoys reading, singing karaoke, playing mermaids in the pool, and doing puzzles.

I love hearing from readers! Check out my socials below or email me at myamorewrites@gmail.com

www.authormyamore.com